PRAISE FOR BRENDA

The MacKenzie Chronic
Brenda Whiteside is known for writing compelling contemporary romantic suspense, but in this one, there's added depth with the historical mystery sub-plot. ~**NN Light's Book Heaven**

This suspenseful, mystery, romance is a page turner. **Still Moments Magazine**

A few very scary moments, wrapped up in a life-long love story, set in scenic Arizona, around a long-lost archaeological site… Hold on – this one is well worth the ride! ~**Paranormal Romance Guild**

Wild Horse Peaks Books (series)
The book's strength is in its characters and descriptions… The setting was a character in itself. ~**Long and Short Reviews**

Brenda Whiteside ropes you in and will have you not moving from your spot until you finish every last page. ~**Page Princess**

The Chocolate Martini Sisters Mystery Books (series)
The who-done-it keeps you guessing each time the sisters discover another clue. This book would fit perfectly in Hallmark's cozy mysteries line-up. ~ **Between the Pages**

From the beginning till the end, there's so much drama (the fun gossipy one) fighting, lovers being exposed, and a bit of a talk about books. ~**Nana's Book Reviews**

…plenty of twists and turns keeping the story fresh and entertaining, coupled with easy-to-read narratives and writing styles… ~**Guatemala Paula**

Sleeping with the Lights On
Cheers to Whiteside for writing a heroine who exists outside of conventional romance novels in terms of age and marital status…novel is written with a pleasantly light sense of humor… ~**RT Book Reviews**

Six quirky Christmas stories sure to brighten your holiday lights.

An Elfin Secret
Candy Cane has never actually seen her father. Could he be Santa Claus? Did her mother have an elf romance? What happens if she's right?

On the Way to the Snow Ball
Nicholas Claus could be delusional, or he might be the sanest person in the elevator. Christmas miracles come when you least expect.

Never Alone on Christmas
After decades of dancing his way from woman to woman, Jonathan Jay Somefun now finds variety-is-the-spice-of-life tasteless. Will this be the Christmas he finds his new style and ends his lonely days?

Love in the Vault
A kiss under the mistletoe, a gun in her ribs, and a lockup in the company vault. If her best friend Cricket arranged this joke, Eleanor will never speak to her again. Or is it a joke?

A Tropical Holiday
Fresh off divorce, Yuma Camry is winging it alone in unreasonably cold Mexico. Whether she's wandering through ghostly Mayan ruins under a cloudy sky or lying on a chilly beach in the bikini she paid too much for, can a stranger with even stranger ideas help her reconnect with herself this Christmas?

No Room at the Inn
Sadi Anne hates Christmas. Volunteering to work through the holiday season is the only way to keep her mind off that heartbreak Christmas three years earlier. But when the hotel loses her reservation, a truck smashes her parked car, and three wisemen come to the rescue, this may be one Christmas she won't want to forget. And neither will the man who broke her heart.

Have Yourself a Quirky Little Christmas

Six Holiday Stories

by
Brenda Whiteside

Brenda Whiteside

This is a work of fiction. Names, characters, places, and incidents are either the product of the author's imagination or are used fictitiously, and any resemblance to actual persons living or dead, business establishments, events, or locales, is entirely coincidental.

Have Yourself a Quirky Little Christmas
Copyright © 2024
Brenda Whiteside

All rights reserved. No part of this book may be used or reproduced in any manner whatsoever without the written permission of the author except in the case of brief quotations embodied in critical articles or reviews.

Cover Design by Alison Henderson
Published in the United States

ISBN: 9798338318034

Acknowledgement

As always, my first nod of thanks goes to my critique partners (in alphabetical order): Tamara Hogan and Heidi M. Thomas. These women are award-winning authors, but they give their time willingly and freely to read every paragraph before I go to print. In addition to being an award-winning author, Heidi is an editor. I'm thankful she edited this book for me.

Dedication

For all those who like stories with a bit of quirk—who see the world in a different light, who are extraordinary, enjoy the outlandish, and are often unconventional.

An Elfin Secret

My mother called him Henry. As far back as I can remember—my third birthday—she spoke of my daddy as if he actually existed.

"Candace, your father, Henry, came while you were sleeping and left you this present for your birthday." She'd clap her hands or kiss my cheek, her face beaming.

Christmas mornings, she'd whisper in my ear at the first sign of dawn. "Your father wants you to have a happy Christmas, and there are presents under the tree from him." The same tag came with every gift, year after year—*I love you, Candy Cane. Be a good girl.*

She spoke of my father like he existed in the same manner Santa Claus existed; only I could see and touch and speak to Santa Claus, at least once a year.

I knew, biologically, that I must have had a father. Even as a five-year-old, I had enough knowledge about the birds and bees to understand the concept of Mommy plus Daddy equals child. I didn't know what Henry looked like, how he sounded or smelled, or what he felt like. There were no pictures or videos of the man my mother loved. Nothing tangible. And no memory.

Only once, when I was five, did I dare question why Daddy didn't live with us. Henry had made another unseen appearance. He'd left a valentine on my pillow while I spun in circles at ballet dance class. I peppered my mother with questions while she made me a peanut butter sandwich. If my daddy couldn't live with us, then why couldn't he be there in my waking hours? Or why couldn't he come before I left for school or still be here when I got home? And didn't we have any pictures of Daddy? Does he love us?

The questions tumbled from me, one after another, until the look on my mother's face scared me so much, my mouth clamped shut, and I held my breath. She'd grown perfectly still, one hand on the Skippy jar and one hand holding the knife loaded with peanut butter in midair above the square of white bread on my blue Smurf plate. Her lips tilted in a half-smile, but no answer issued from them. Her cheeks grew rosy. The sparkle in her blue eyes stilled. Her face froze in time like a beautiful marble bust. She stared, not seeing me, and I wanted to yell, "I take it back! I take it back!" Instead, I asked for milk with my peanut butter sandwich. The words took her off pause. Her face relaxed, and the knife with peanut butter continued its journey down to the bread.

We returned to our usual routine.

Henry left me gifts, my thanks delivered via my mother. I couldn't bear the thought of ever again causing Mommy— a gentle, cheerful soul—the bafflement I'd witnessed. And the reaction had scared me. Who could this man be who would leave me gifts and loved me but whose existence was such a guarded secret that disclosing anything more rendered my mother near comatose?

It must have been sometime around the peanut butter episode, as I came to remember it, when Henry and Santa Claus merged. They had so much in common: gift giving, undisclosed source of income, magical properties, unconditional love, secretive. Lying in bed with only the Cinderella nightlight glowing, casting faint shadows across the white canopy overhead, I thought about my father, Henry. What would my father look like? His smile came first. Daddy would have to be happy, giving me gifts all the time. And then the eyes. He'd have sparkly, blue eyes like Mommy, and they'd crinkle when he smiled. I could see his eyes dancing above me in the white canopy, and so he took on a white beard and fluff of hair.

When my mother took me to see Santa Claus at the mall, I realized Daddy and Santa could possibly be the same person. It explained his absence from our everyday lives. Santa couldn't live among normal people. And he'd be far too busy all year getting ready for Christmas all over the world. Henry couldn't be Santa Claus *and* live in Minneapolis, Minnesota. Plus, no child ever *saw* Santa in her house. Santa made his visits at Christmas, and you had to believe he existed because he left behind presents, just like Henry did for me on all those special occasions. And even though he was my father, Santa Claus couldn't reveal himself—even to his daughter. He didn't reveal himself at the mall either. Mother had explained on my first visit how Santa used doubles, but I could be sure that the real Santa got my messages.

His secret remained safe with me. I'd never had a father at the spring choral presentations or on field days, but I didn't feel slighted. Mommy always took his place, happy and laughing. My father, Santa, not only made midnight visits to me on Christmas like he did for all the children of the world, he made stealth visits to *me* all year long. Pure magic. The secret made me special.

"Happy birthday, Candace." My mother woke me on my sixth birthday. The curtains swished open, and sun poured in my room. "I had strict orders from your father to wake you and give you his present at exactly five minutes to seven." She sat at the foot of my bed. "Come on, sleepy girl.

It's the magic hour."

"What do you mean, Mommy?" I rubbed my eyes and brushed tangles of hair from my face.

She pinched my toes through the spread, wiggling my feet. "If your father says seven is the hour to open what's inside this box, we'll make it the magic hour."

I sat and scooted closer to her, covers bunching around my legs. She laid the square package in my lap. "But Mommy, you can't just make magic."

"No, Candace, I can't, but maybe we can together." She checked her wristwatch, then tapped the present. "Open your gift."

The paper around the present, so light and translucent, floated off with a slight touch from my fingers. I glanced at my mother, but she didn't look at all concerned. When I lifted the book, she scooped the paper from my lap. In *her* hands, the wrapping paper crunched white and opaque, as she wadded it to throw away.

The front of the book glittered and glowed, and although sizable for my small hands to hold, felt light as a feather. One word adorned the cover, *Elves*.

Mommy quirked a brow. "What an interesting looking book. It's very old." The blue bird clock beside my bed chimed seven. Her breath swirled the air around me when she whispered, "You're to open it at precisely seven o'clock. Open it."

The book didn't appear old to me, but then at six, maybe I didn't know old from new when it came to books. I lifted the cover. Inside were pictures of elves in every imaginable setting and mode of dress. The pictures were totally engaging, and I slowly turned each page, mesmerized.

"Hmm," my mother murmured. "No words. Well, that's a funny book. I don't suppose there's much to learn from a picture book, but it's pretty to look at."

I gazed at a red-suited, plump elf whose identity needed no caption. He winked. I gasped and looked at Mommy, but she hadn't noticed. Or didn't make a face or bat an eye if she'd noticed.

"Mommy?"

"Hmm?"

"Santa is his first name and Claus is his last name. My name is Candace Cane. What is Henry's last name?"

"Cane, sweetheart."

"That's his people name?"

"Yes." She smiled. "You're a wise little girl."

"But why—"

"I'll go make breakfast, birthday girl." She patted my leg and left my room, closing the door behind her.

I stared at the book in my lap. Mommy's description of my picture book hadn't been exactly correct. Maybe no words jumped off the page to be read, but they were there to be absorbed. Yet not all at once. This particular day, in addition to the wink which told me the book held secrets for me alone, I also learned an education in the way of elves would be ladled out in rationed amounts, slowly, each year on my birthday.

Lesson One: Learn to Keep Secrets.

But holding this secret brought me near to bursting about my magic book, magic only I could see.

"Mommy, did you see any magic in my book?" I asked as I spooned gobs of frosty cake into my mouth.

"Magic? Well, I didn't *see* any magic, but then it's not my book." She handed me a napkin. "I think real magic is a personal thing. Oh, there's magic like pulling rabbits out of hats. But *real* magic, it's different things to different people."

What good was personal magic if no one else could see

it?

The warnings of *Lesson One: Learn to Keep Secrets*, issued quietly every time I touched the book but were easily ignored while I played in the front yard with Sarah.

"I have a secret, Sarah. Come on." We climbed the stairs, my heart thumping harder with each step closer to my room. Once inside I closed the door and beamed. "You see?"

"What?"

How could she miss the glow coming from my toy shelf? "The book. Isn't it beautiful?"

She followed the direction I pointed. "I see a book, but it looks like any other book. So what?"

I ran to the shelf and lifted the tome without effort. Hardly touching my fingers, my gift floated against the palms of my hands. "Touch it."

Sarah screwed her mouth to the side and poked the book. "Yeah, now what? Where's the secret?"

"Hold it."

"*Elves*. Sounds neat." She took the book from me with one hand, but in her hand the weight matched the size, and she nearly dropped it. She plopped down to the floor and flipped open the cover.

I sat beside her, excitement tingling my scalp and giddiness bathing me as I fidgeted. "Look." She'd come to the picture of Santa Claus.

Sarah gave me a sideways scowl like I'd lost my wits.

"Don't you see?"

"Jeez, Candace, you're acting goofy."

"Magic, Sarah." I'd thought someone my own age might share the excitement. "Don't you see it?"

"See what?"

"The magic." My giddiness dissolved as I stared into the eyes of Santa. He didn't wink.

Sarah slapped the cover shut. "Yeah, well, magic's the

word my mom always uses when she talks about Santa, but I'm not sure he even exists. And you act like you've never seen a picture of him before."

"It's…it's not just him. It's the book."

"The book is magic?" She cocked her head, picked the cover up and let it drop back. "How?"

"It's different."

"It's a heavy, old, brown book. It's not even new or very pretty. Where'd you get it, the library?"

The book, neither old or brown, shimmered blue and floated a miniscule degree atop my carpet. "Never mind." I scooped it up and the volume drifted from my hand to the shelf. "Just never mind."

Lesson learned.

And life and the pattern of visits from my father, Henry, continued.

New toys, dance, and school occupied me more than books. *Elves* collected dust on my shelf for a year. Whenever I received a present from my father, I'd give a cursory glance at the book, but the pictures were flat and quiet from a distance, so I left it on the shelf.

At a few minutes before seven o'clock, I awoke on the morning of my seventh birthday. My eyes popped open to the sound of my name. Expecting my mother to grab my toes and wish me a happy birthday, I waited. When nothing happened, I raised my head from the pillow and looked around. Mommy stood in front of my bookcase as still as my Chatty Cathy next to my collection of music boxes. In the dim room, only my book glowed from my shelf, beckoning me.

"Mommy?"

"Yes, Candace." She still hadn't moved.

"Mommy, did you call me?"

"No, honey."

"What are you doing?"

She continued to stare at the bookshelf.

"Did you want to read my book?"

As if her switch had been flipped, her body came to life, and she whirled around, grabbed my toes beneath the covers, and sang, "Happy birthday to you, happy birthday to you, happy birthday dear Candace, happy birthday to you."

I clapped my hands, and she climbed under the covers and tickled me until I screamed uncle.

"You're such a pretty girl." She brushed the hair out of my eyes. "I'll call you when the hotcakes are ready, and you can open your gift from your father before you eat. You don't get mine until your party on Saturday."

After she closed my door, I considered climbing out of bed to get the book and curling up beneath my covers to turn the pages, something I'd not done for nearly a year. When my effort to share the magic with Sarah had fallen flat, I'd more or less neglected my treasured, magic gift. The idea had no more left my head when my clock chimed seven, and I found myself in exactly the position I thought of. The book lay in my lap, my hands on the book's cover. No longer awed by what only I could see, I opened the book and absorbed the next lesson.

Lesson Two: The Bridge. A term used for a human who is a link to the Elfin world. Bridges interact with Elves in such a way they accept the interaction without question. They're like a carrier of power but never acquire the power. Bridges can mate with Elves to create Halflings.

Bridges are very special humans. The keeper of secrets. Their love is endless, their acceptance unending, their joy eternal. They are extremely rare. All Halflings require connection through a Bridge until their fifteenth year.

This new-found knowledge seeped into me gently, but no matter how gentle the intention, once I fully understood and grasped the meaning, it hit me like a lightning strike. I fell back onto my pillow and gasped. Then bolted upright and began flipping pages wildly, begging for more information. I didn't understand. My mother was a Bridge, and that made me a Halfling. What did this mean? I was half an Elf, half a Santa named Henry? What would happen on my fifteenth birthday? I flipped and scanned for a few minutes but in vain. At last, calmness returned as I leafed through pages, transfixed by the pictures of funny elves, pretty elves, serious elves, elves of all sizes and manner of dress until the page turning landed on Santa Claus's face again. The wink. The secret.

My eighth and ninth birthdays came, more lessons learned.

Lesson Three: Elfen History. Elves long ago embraced earth and humans, and in so doing adapted to the dominant race of Earthlings. Elves retain their magical powers and are closer to nature than humans, as they live beside rather than within the human race. Humans, living beside the Elfin population but on a different plane of understanding, have the ability to explain away any Elfin behavior or magic they witness. The human exception is the Bridge. A Bridge sees both planes and accepts without the knowledge to explain.

Lesson Four: The Years Are Important: At the age of eleven, a Halfling should be almost fully educated in the ways of Elves. On her eleventh birthday, a Halfling must choose to become an Elf or remain a human.

Each lesson ended with the wink. The secret.
The morning of my tenth birthday, I woke to Mommy humming. The familiar tune floated up the stairs and into my

room through the opened door. I called to my Elf book, and it glided onto my bed. I waited, gazing at my bluebird clock. On the seventh chime, the cover of my book opened.

Lesson Five: An Important Choice. On her eleventh birthday, if the Halfling does not make a conscious decision to become an Elf wholly, she will remain human. The Halfling who remains human, will be human in most ways, such as number of years lived, but will retain some magical powers of extended sight. From her eleventh birthday to her fifteenth year, the Halfling, whether human or Elf, will remain connected to the Elfin world through her Bridge. In her fifteenth year, if she has chosen to be Elf wholly, she will transition to the Elfin world, but if she is human, she will bid farewell to Elfin possibilities. She'll retain the magic of extended sight.

Mommy's humming grew louder as she appeared in my doorway. "Good morning, Candace. Happy tenth birthday. Are you excited about going to the skating rink this afternoon? Sarah must be. She called a few minutes ago."

"Mmm…yeah." I couldn't take my eyes from my book.

"You never tire of your picture book, do you? That's probably the best present your father, Henry, ever gave you." She stood over me gazing at the book.

Her warm hand glided down my cheek, and I peered into her eyes. "Do you miss him, Mommy?"

"Miss him?" She sat at the foot of my bed.

There must have been a time when Henry did more in this house than drop off presents. Somehow, they must have spent a lot of time together, I thought, or I wouldn't be there. "Like when you were together?"

"Were? Candace, you talk as if he's in the past. Your father's always with us."

"Not really."

Her brow wrinkled. Confusion clouded her face. "Yes,

always. He's always here, in a way, and at other times in another way. Not in the sense Sarah's father is or…or… Oh! Candace, I seem to be short on words."

"Why do you call him Henry?"

She tilted her head. Her blue eyes grew gray. "Candace, you ask the most unusual questions." She stood. The stone expression I remembered from a few years back flickered across her face.

My heart thumped, and I rose to my knees, but before I could apologize, tell her never mind, the twinkle in her eyes danced. "Your father is a very special father. Which makes you a very special person. Oh, if only I were so special. He loves me. His love fills me with happiness. What we share is…" She waved a hand in the air.

"You don't know you're special, Mommy?"

She sat, drawing me closer this time. "I'm different." A giggle escaped, and she touched my cheek. "You're still a little too young to understand. Although I have to say, you've always been wiser than you should be. *You've* always been wise, and *I've* always been *different*. I crossed a bridge one night on Christmas nearly eleven years ago." She sighed and smiled. "And look what I have. My life is like a fairy tale."

"Happily ever after."

"See how wise you are?" She patted my leg and stood. "Now, get dressed and come down to breakfast."

I glanced at my book, open on the Santa Claus page. The wink. The secret.

I became exceptionally good at keeping secrets but not as good as my mother. One winter morning, two weeks before Christmas and three weeks before my eleventh birthday, I woke to the sun streaming in my bedroom. My eyelids lifted and the white of the canopy over my bed nearly blinded me with the brightness of a new day. It had snowed for several days during the week, and now, a sunny Saturday morning would be perfect for sledding before we made our annual trip to see Santa. Santa Saturday.

Racing down the stairs to the kitchen, I stopped halfway and listened. Nothing but quiet. No kitchen noises.

"Mommy?" I took one more step down.

"Mommy?" I took two steps back up. Over my shoulder, I saw her closed bedroom door.

"Mommy?" My bare feet padded quietly along the hall to her bedroom. I put my ear to the door as I grabbed the doorknob.

"Candace," she whispered.

I opened the door and peered into the bedroom, shrouded in semi-darkness by curtained windows. My mother's eyes were closed, but she raised a hand and one finger motioned for me to come closer. This was foreign territory. Our home had always been bright; my mother never seemed to sleep. She worked and cleaned and cooked and drove me to school and dance. She hummed and laughed. Lying in bed on Santa Saturday in a dark room meant something.

I put my hand on her shoulder so she would know I stood beside her.

"Are you sick, Mommy?"

"I'm sorry, Candace."

"It's okay. We can go see Santa tomorrow."

She turned her head. The pillow relaxed and cradled her face as she opened her eyes. Her lashes were thick, and I remember thinking how slow her eyes opened because her lashes must be very heavy.

"Call Auntie Helen. Okay? Can you do that?"

I nodded and rubbed her shoulder.

"Tell Auntie Helen. Tell Auntie Helen...it's time."

"Time for what, Mommy?"

"Go call Auntie. Now." She closed her eyes.

I moved my hand to her face and stroked her forehead like she would do to me when I lay sick. Her hand came up, took my hand, and pressed it to her lips.

I tiptoed out of her room, then ran down the stairs to the only telephone in our house, in the kitchen. My hand shook as I dialed the number. It took me two times to get the number right. Auntie Helen and Uncle Rutie lived five houses down on the same side of the street, but at the curve of the cul-de-sac. We could see their house from our upstairs windows.

Auntie said, "Oh dear child," when I repeated what my mother had said to say.

"Can you put the kettle on for tea, Candace?"

"Yes, but…"

"You put the kettle on because Uncle Rutie hasn't had his morning tea, and he really must."

"But Auntie…"

"And take the butter out of the fridge so it will get soft for toast. He likes toast with his tea. I'm putting on my shoes and coat right now. You stay in the kitchen and get those things ready, and we'll be there in two minutes. Hurry up, Rutie! You can do what I asked, can't you, Candace?"

Auntie, my mother's older sister by ten years, seemed ancient compared to my mother. Where my mother was spontaneous and laughed a great deal, Auntie Helen loved routine and rarely laughed out loud when a smile would do. They were alike only in their ability to keep secrets.

****

My world changed.

My father's life and my mother's death remained mysteries.

I moved into my relatives' quiet, plain home five doors down and watched my old life disappear when the For Sale sign went up in my front yard.

There was no Santa Saturday that year. My mother died, and the why and how remained as much a secret to me as why I never saw my father, Henry.

Christmas came and went as a backdrop to the funeral and mourning. There didn't seem to be a moment to request a visit to Santa, so three days before Christmas I wrote him a letter. I told him Mommy had died. I asked if he could come see me. A real visit from my father would be all I needed for Christmas. I had no idea how to get it to him, so I asked Auntie to mail it special for me. She stoically watched as I sealed the letter, then wrote in giant print, "Santa or you know who." She tucked it in the pocket of her yellow apron with only a fleeting puzzled expression.

Christmas morning dawned quiet and solemn. There were presents under the tree for me—two from Auntie and Uncle Rutie, three from Santa. The tags and paper were all the same. There were none from Henry. No presents for *Candy Cane*.

"Do you know my father, Henry Cane?" I asked as we opened the puzzle box Uncle Rutie had given me. My uncle looked at Auntie.

"No, Candace." She spread the puzzle pieces on the coffee table. "We never knew your father. Oh my, look at all these pieces. This is going to take a while!"

"Auntie…"

"You know, Candace, some questions just don't have answers which satisfy little girls." She patted my hand. "How 'bout you start the milk for some hot chocolate? Figuring out a puzzle goes so much smoother with a cup of hot chocolate in your hand."

Later, while Auntie quilted in the basement and Uncle Rutie watched television, I sat by the window in my cozy attic bedroom and tried to make sense of it. Maybe my letter didn't get to him in time. Maybe Daddy saw the For Sale sign and thought we moved without telling him. But the Santa part of my father, the magical part, should have known where to find me. Tears streamed down my face. My chest ached with longing for my mother.

While my tears dried, a plan evolved. I needed to leave a note at my old house and tell Henry where I lived now. From his easy chair in front of the television, Uncle Rutie would be able to see me go out the front door, so I tiptoed across the linoleum kitchen floor, being careful to step around the squeaky spot in front of the stove. I opened the back door enough to squeeze out so no cold draft would alert my uncle. I trotted across the back yards of the houses between my new home and my old one. Wedging the note in the door jamb of the front door lifted my spirits.

With a hopeful attitude, I skipped and jumped along the street. When I cut by the side of the house to the kitchen door, a blue lump on our front stoop, lightly dusted with snow, caught my attention.

My heart pounded with a joy I'd not felt for weeks. For a moment, I clutched the gift to my chest with both hands, tears filling my eyes. When I finally got over the wonder of the moment, I tore open the wrapping. Inside, a small framed picture of a young woman looking into the face of Santa puzzled me. The size of the picture made it hard to clearly see the woman. I stepped from under the eave so the light would help. *Mommy*. Younger but, without a doubt, my mother. My breath caught. The gaze between my mother and Santa couldn't be mistaken. As if they'd just kissed, her cheeks glowed and the twinkle in his eye had nothing to do with leaving presents for children of the world.

Back in my bedroom and by the window, I could see the corner of the note in the front door of my old house. I clutched the picture Henry left in my hand. Lesson One whispered across my mind. The secret.

The next morning, I sprang from my bed as if Christmas morning came a second time. I hopped to the window. When I saw the note gone, I clapped my hands and giggled with joy. All I had to do now was wait.

I wondered what to do while I waited. And the book came to mind. I hadn't seen it since I'd moved into my new bedroom. My closet held a couple of unpacked boxes, and I rummaged through them until a faint light glowed. Huddled in the closet between the boxes, legs crossed, I carefully turned each page waiting for more Elfin wisdom. Surely I needed to know what to do now that Mommy had left me. There must be a clue, even if I still had a week until my birthday. I flipped the pages, but nothing came. A wall went up in my mind as if all I'd learned resided within me on one side of the wall and something more whispered to me from the other side. But I couldn't hear. I packed the book back into the box, shoved it to the far corner of the closet, and closed the door.

The clouds grew dark while I stayed glued to my window. Waiting.

Henry never came.

On the morning of my eleventh birthday, I awoke a few minutes before seven. The morning, joyless and flat, like the week of mornings since I'd left the note for Henry, lay before me. I took the picture of my mother and Santa from where I'd wedged it between the mattress and the headboard. I could take the book from the box, but without my mother, my Bridge, the wonder of the magic had paled. The disappointment weighed like a gray brick on my chest, keeping me from moving. My eleventh birthday was supposed to be some great moment of decision. Human or Elf? *Elves aren't always here when you need them.* I would stay human. My bluebird clock chimed seven. After tucking the picture into its hiding place, I covered my head and went back to sleep.

At eight, I woke again feeling out of sorts, with the nagging dread of having missed something. All day, I moped. The hours dragged on while Auntie and Uncle constantly tried to cheer me. The enormous cake had colorful decorations, and they gave me not one but three presents. But no present from my father, Henry, waited with the gifts.

Maybe Henry didn't exist after all. He stopped existing when Mommy stopped existing. Maybe the present of the picture had been there all along—a gift from my mother, dropped in the snow when Auntie and Uncle moved everything from the house. There hadn't been a tag identifying the giver.

As I grew older and my friends stopped believing in Santa, I accepted Santa Claus as a fantasy to leave behind with childhood. I stopped wondering about Henry. His existence faded rather than coming to a grand halt the way Santa's had. The book lay dormant in the bottom of the box of childhood toys. The glow had ceased.

In the winter, two weeks before Christmas on Santa Saturday, when I was fifteen, Sarah, Karen, and I shopped the mall. I looked for a tie for Uncle Rutie.

"My dad might like this one." Sarah held up a red and blue striped tie.

"Where's your father, Candace? You never talk about him," Karen asked as she fingered the ties hanging from the rack.

"The North Pole."

"What?"

"The North Pole." Sarah and Karen looked at me as if waiting for the punch line to a joke. "May as well be the North Pole. I've never seen him."

"Never seen him, but do you know who he is?" Karen,

the persistent kind, continued to quiz me.

"He used to stop by and leave me presents before my mom died, but I never actually saw him." I moved along the counter, putting space between myself and my friends. How stupid to volunteer such information. Karen would want the whole story. My insides trembled and anger and sadness collided.

When Karen made a move toward me, Sarah caught her sleeve. Sarah, the sensitive one, would give me space.

"So don't you want to find him?" Karen frowned and tugged away from our friend.

I shrugged, and my eyes burned.

"It's been how many years since your mom died?"

"Five. And so what?" An ache tore at my chest, an ache remembered from years ago. "He didn't want to find me, so who needs a father anyway? He's like Santa Claus. When you grow up, he no longer exists." I dropped the ties I'd been considering. "I have to go to the bathroom. I'll be back in a minute."

I practically ran down the aisle and around the counter to the bathrooms. My reaction to the conversation surprised me as much as how I'd blabbered on about my father, Henry. I made my way through racks and counters of flowing colors blurring together through watery tears until I bumped into a mound of soft red.

"Ho, there young lady." The voice rang musical and deep. "Can I help you?"

My gaze followed red to a fluff of white. I wiped away tears and gazed into smiling blue eyes, the skin crinkled at the corners, and a wide smile I recognized.

"Henry?"

"Shh! Santa's my name." He put his finger to my chin and winked. "Have you forgotten Lesson One already?"

Learn to keep secrets. My heart raced, and I couldn't speak.

I blinked more tears away, but he didn't blink away with them.

"If you were a little younger and a little shorter, I might think you'd lost your mother and need help." He tilted his head to one side and questioned me with those jolly eyes.

"I did lose my mother. Five years ago." I sniffed.

His finger left my chin and brushed along my face. His kindness didn't lessen my angry sadness.

"I lost my mother, Henry, and Santa all the same year."

He nodded. "A very rough year for you." His hands were behind his back now, and he seemed to rock on his heels, staring into my face all the while.

"You knew."

His sigh was as heavy as his belly. "We aren't lost, Candy Cane."

"You knew, and you didn't come." I swiped at my face, no longer wanting to make a display of sadness to my absentee father.

"I was there."

"No, you weren't." My shoulders trembled. "You're my father, yet you didn't come."

"You might not have seen me, Candy Cane, but I was there." He touched my cheek. "And you made the choice…slipped into the human realm."

"I was lost without my mother. My choice? *You* could have done something."

His rosy cheeks paled. "Some things are meant to be."

"Like losing my mother."

"I have no answers for you on some things, Candy Cane." He glanced side to side, then a mist swirled around us. "Close your eyes. Good. Now remember the lessons as best you can and the touch of magic you will always have."

As if my feet left the ground, I floated in a cloud. Elfin words rang in my ears, and a whisper of the teachings brushed across my mind. I nodded. In the mists behind my eyelids, my mother's youthful face appeared. She smiled sweetly. Her soft lips touched my forehead. We spoke without words and then she vanished. I opened my eyes to the man in red, the mist surrounding us.

"I miss her."

"Yes."

"Is that all you have to say?" The mist grew lighter.

"There are paths to follow, the ways not always clearly marked. And paths take turns we don't always expect." He waved his hand above his head. The mist grew heavy again.

"Why are you here now?" A tear toppled down my cheek.

"To remind you."

"Of what?"

"That love never dies, my sweet child. And of your Halfling abilities."

A flood of memories swirled in the mist around me. My magical extended sight would keep my mother and my father with me forever.

"Remember your magic, but use it sparingly." Putting his finger under my chin again, his smile broadened. "When you go home, look in the mirror. We are in your heart, and we are part of you. You'll see us. Look closely, and you'll have us forever, Candy Cane."

"Candace!" Karen and Sarah shouted my name at the same time. I whirled around as they clamored to my side.

"What's taking you so long? Are you okay?" Sarah touched my shoulder.

"I just…" I motioned to explain the presence of Santa, but racks of clothing stood behind me.

"Are you crying?" Karen asked. "What's wrong?"

"Did you see him?" I did a pirouette, scanning in every direction.

"See who?" They stood on each side of me following my searching gaze.

My father.

"Come on." I had to find him again. "Let's go see Santa!"

I ran through the store to the escalator, Karen and Sarah close behind, throwing questions at me as to why I wanted to see Santa. I bounded down the escalator, brushing past Christmas shoppers with bags and small children in tow, heading for the children's department, on a mission to finish the conversation with Santa. I slowed when the holiday scene came into view, him sitting in his overstuffed red velvet chair, a thin elf in green standing by his side. The little boy on his lap looked shy as Santa Claus spoke quietly and smiled. When he set the child down, his gaze landed on me standing by the rope dividing his area from the aisle.

He wasn't my Santa.

"Where is he?" I shouted across the green carpeted area. "Where is he?"

The green clad elf, bells jingling on her pointy-toed shoes, answered. "Who are you looking for?"

"The other Santa. The real one."

"Shush. There's only one Santa." She leaned across the rope. Up close, an elderly lady, thin and wiry filled the elf suit. She whispered, "There are little kids here, and this is Santa."

"Is there another one? Another Santa in this store?"

"No, dear. This is the only Santa at the mall. He's been doing this for years."

Of course he had. He was one of the doubles Mommy had explained to me years ago. I stepped back from the rope and faced my friends. They each grabbed one of my arms and led me away from the Santa crowd.

"What the heck is going on with you?" Karen frowned

at me like I'd gone half-crazed.

Sarah rubbed my arm. "Candace, you're acting weird. You haven't acted this weird since you know when. You know—with the book. Are you okay?"

A vision of the book, at the bottom of a box in my closet, made me smile. "I am. I'm fine."

"Tell us what's going on so we can get on with shopping." Karen popped her gum and had her hands on her hips.

"Way too much to explain," I said. "It's history. And I can live with that. I can finally live with all of it." I couldn't explain my father Henry's elf name was Santa. I couldn't explain my mother the Bridge, and I'd never explain I was a Halfling. Secrets. *Lesson One: Learn to Keep Secrets.* "Let's go find a tie."

I found my magic and my father again when I was fifteen. My mother is in my heart, and I visit her occasionally. And I'm still a good keeper of secrets. I still believe in Santa Claus. My children don't, but that's okay. Someday, when they're old enough to understand, I'll tell them the truth about Santa—show them the photo of Grandma and Henry—and they can believe all over again.

On the Way to the Snow Ball

Pulling this off would take a Christmas miracle.

With an excited tremor, Nicholas punched the lobby button on the elevator keyboard. Twenty-four floors, then through the glass doors, and into a cab to arrive at the Snow Ball. His pulse kicked up as the doors glided toward each other. But visions of making his grand entrance into the ball flitted away when a small, manicured hand thrust through the sliver of an opening and bounced the doors apart.

He retreated to the back of the cube as the young woman—or was she a girl?—hopped onto the elevator. *Ignore her. She won't know me or where I'm going and can't hinder my mission.*

Rocking a moment on the balls of her feet clad in shiny, black heels, she smiled—one of those brief, close-mouthed, polite smiles as the hallway disappeared and she shifted, turning away from him. A subtle, electrical hum indicated they were moving.

Twenty-four, Twenty-three.

A distant screech of scraping metal nearly drowned out the whisper of the ebony-haired girl. "What was that?"

He gripped the railing on the back wall with one hand while adjusting his white, fur-trimmed, red hat with his other. The old elevator always groaned. Glints of light from the track around the top edges of the elevator played across the back of her hair, a reflection moving like the wave a crowd does at a football game. *Hmm, how long had it been since he'd been to a ball game? Decades, maybe.*

Another creak, and she jumped. "Why have we stopped?" She darted a glance in his direction. "Hey, what happened to the lights?"

The darkness was blacker than a moonless night at the North Pole.

His heart thumped against his ribs. Small spaces didn't bother him. He lived in a small space with small people. But an elevator malfunction would disrupt his plan. *Patience.*

She shuffled her feet. "It's so quiet."

"Don't worry." The young person needed reassuring. "Someone will fix it." He leaned his hips against the railing that ran along the walls, the cold metal chilling his bottom through his red dress slacks. The dark was so thick, so silent, if he'd not seen her before the lights went out, he'd think he was alone. Except for her annoying, spicy scent. The smell made his nose itch.

A distant growl of metal echoed from far below them. A gasp from his unseen companion bounced around the blackness.

"Don't panic," he offered. "How are we doing?"

"Fine, if getting stuck in a dark elevator with a stranger is your idea of fun." Her caustic tone could indicate fear.

"Although, I'm perfectly harmless. There's no need for alarm." He swallowed deeply. He never wanted to frighten anyone.

"Of course there isn't. I have a black belt in karate."

"Then you can protect both of us, should the need arise." He knew how to handle unforeseen situations. "No reason to get excited." His reassurances should have a calming effect.

"This is hardly exciting, and I'm not afraid of the dark."

"Just stay calm!" So much for requiring his reassurance. "I'm only trying to help."

"All right, all right." The blackness didn't mute her huff.

He imagined her arms crossed, and her eyes glaring. Young people nowadays didn't have many social skills. All that technology kept them in the dark. *The dark. Good one.* He ran a finger between his neck and the collar of his shirt. The space grew stuffy. He should've been on his way out of the building. He needed a Christmas miracle, and what he got instead was an obstacle.

"But what do you think is going on?" Her voice, now quietly needy, slithered between his thoughts.

"It's probably a power problem."

"Oh, really?"

Her sarcasm wasn't quiet. He could ignore it.

"We should call for help," she suggested. "I left my cell in my purse in the office. Do you have yours?"

"No." Cell phones, email, and electronic voices. He shuddered. Why would he want to be reached wherever he went? *All messages are delivered to the workshop.* That was their job. He only checked them—twice.

"Hey, wait!" Her sudden outburst made him straighten up from his resting-place on the railing. "The telephone! All elevators have telephones. It must be on this side by the buttons." Her scuffling noises shattered the dark.

"Stop. You might touch something you shouldn't." He took a few steps in the direction of the sounds of her movements and was startled when he bumped into her. "Oh sorry! Excuse me, but please don't touch anything."

"I'm looking for the phone."

"Tell me what you find before you actually do anything." Only inches from her, the pitch-black took on her irritating scent. His nose twitched, and he took a breath through his mouth. The black air grew warmer. He loosened his tie.

"I feel a metal door. This has to be it. Too bad I don't read Braille."

"Here, let me see." He reached out, amazed when his hand found the small oblong metal door as she opened it.

"I can do it!" An elbow knocked his hand away. "I'm perfectly capable of speaking on a telephone."

"Of course, you're capable." How could he deal with such childishness? Yet, his lot in life was exactly that. Granted, the younger ones were so much easier to contain, to appease, to please before they grew into double-digit ages.

"Hello, hello. There's no sound. No dial tone or anything. Hello!" This time she screamed.

He wiped the dampness from his forehead. Excitement, overzealous joy he could handle, not panic. "Now, will you let *me* have it?"

A hard thump hit his chest as she relinquished the phone. In his ear, there was silence, dead silence. With his other hand, he ran fingers around the perimeter of the box and along the back. Cold metal. His nails snagged on six screws. Nothing else. He'd never used an elevator phone. Never given any thought as to how they operated. Maybe it was there for looks only, giving a false sense of security to the occupants, like the pretend cameras or plastic phones he delivered. Or it might be an alarm to catch you for touching something you shouldn't. His hand jerked back. He fumbled, setting the receiver back on its cradle.

"Maybe it sets off an alarm when you pick it up. Just wait." Nothing. How long should he wait? There was a crackle overhead. The Carpenters harmonized, "Away in a Manger." At least *something* was fixed.

"This is progress, right?" Her voice sounded hopeful.

Setting his finger aside of his nose, he raised his gaze upward, but only black met him. He wondered if a panel in the ceiling could be slid away.

"Right?"

"Hmm…yes, progress." He'd nearly forgotten about her with his musings.

Overhead the lights flickered, went out, then shone and held. Although dim, his relief flashed bright.

Her dark brown eyes widened as she scanned their surroundings as if searching, for what? More people? She bit her dark red lower lip, which clashed with her neon orange dress. He didn't like orange, a poor imitation of red.

"Well!" She tilted her chin in his direction. "Music. Lights. Now where's the camera? Since when doesn't an elevator have a security camera?"

He surveyed every corner. She was right. After two years, or was it four years, going in and out of this building, he had never noticed there weren't cameras in the elevators. They must be hidden. No good watching people if they knew you were watching.

She walked around the compartment, corner to corner. "It may be my imagination, but I think this contraption is broken." Sarcasm again.

"Well, it certainly isn't moving." He tried to match her wit.

"Do you think it could fall?"

"It isn't even moving."

"But, do you think if I were to move around too much, it would fall?"

His abilities might be taxed in dealing with her. His skills had been limited to reaffirming belief—fireside chats with children—not survival techniques for young adults. Where was his Christmas miracle? "No, of course not."

"How do you know?"

He gave her his most authoritative expression. He hoped. Jolly wouldn't work in this instance. "It's easy to get upset in such situations."

She cocked her head to one side. "Do I *look* like I'm upset?"

He stroked his close-cropped beard, still unhappy about having to cut it. He stared at a sassy smile on a pale face dusted with freckles. He opened his mouth to answer when the elevator gave a jolt. Knocked off balance, he stumbled and caught himself on the metal railing.

The young woman gasped, but kept her balance, throwing her hands to her chest. He saw the time on her watch. Damn. They'd miss him at the Snow Ball, and they'd come looking. The elevator creaked, the lights flickered, and the dark enveloped them again.

"They must be trying to fix it." She sounded hopeful.

He stood perfectly still, listening for noise beyond their breathing, but the only sound was Barry Manilow crooning overhead.

"Kill. The. Elevator. *Music.*" Each word rose in pitch until she was screeching. "Why play music if the stupid thing isn't moving?"

He understood her irritation. "Jingle Bells" should not be crooned.

Again, the lights blinked and this time stayed on, dimmer than before. His eyes adjusted to the semi-darkness. Agitation wrinkled her forehead.

Despite their situation, joy should fill their lives, not needless negative moodiness. His plans could fall through, but he should be jolly. He swallowed, ill-equipped to deal with her age group, but he'd give it a shot. "Does the music upset you?"

"It makes me manic!" She threw her hands in the air.

At her mischievous smile, Nicholas made a snap evaluation. Not particularly rational to do so, yet under the current circumstances, he'd learned a good deal in a short span of time about the needy, insecure young lady.

She paced in front of the elevator door.

"Are you—?" Her scent tickled his nose again. "Are you claustro…claustrophobic?" He sneezed the last word.

"Are you allergic to elevators?"

"I think I'm allergic to you." Allergic reactions were caused by the body trying to defend itself against a suspected harmful entity. Ridiculous. She was just a very young person—of no harm to him. What had led him to those thoughts. *Oh yes.* "What have you got on? The scent?"

"A special holiday blend. Cinnamon and pine needles."

No wonder. Who'd decided these things equated to the smell of Christmas? They might have asked him what the real scent of Christmas was before deciding. He removed the jacket of his red suit and loosened his tie. Neatly folding the jacket, he draped it over a section of the metal railing.

"That's quite a suit."

"Thank you."

She snickered. "I'll give it to you—takes confidence to wear something like that. Even this time of year."

"You don't like it?"

She ran a quick glance over him, hat to shoes. When she came back for a second look, she paused on his face. "Actually, I do. I mean the cut is good. You're well-built so that helps to carry it off. Not sure about the Santa hat. But I guess it's the season."

"So, if I wore this some other time of year, you might reconsider your opinion?" He didn't need her opinion, but something about her approval affected him like sweet caramel apples. Mmm…caramel apples. They were sure to serve those again this year at the Snow Ball.

"Do you dress like this *all* the time?" A sharp squeal, this time overhead, wiped the tease from her face.

Jarred back to reality, his need to escape before they found him returned. *Miracle. Concentrate on a miracle.*

"So." The girl broke into his worry. "I wonder why the elevator just quit."

"I've been in and out of this building for years, and it's never happened before."

"There's always a reason for things happening." She gave him a half smile. "Nothing just happens."

She was right. Quite intuitive. People who believed in chance were kidding themselves.

With narrowed eyes, she tipped her chin downward. "Maybe it's sabotage."

Her tone joked, but she might've actually hit on something. "Maybe it's..." *Couldn't be a coincidence.* "A patient. A patient who doesn't like the way his sessions are going. And he's a retired electrician." The man insisted on calling him Harry when they met in group. They didn't get along.

"Are you a shrink or something? From the clinic in the suite of offices on the twenty-fourth floor?"

He studied her studying him. "What if I am? And please don't say shrink." He couldn't tolerate disrespect. He had to stay focused on getting out of here. Yet...why was this girl thrown into his path? She had yet to ask for anything, but she must need something.

"I've never met a *shrink*."

Clearly, she meant to push his buttons. He rolled up the sleeves of his white dress shirt and ignored her insolence. "I'll be missed at the Snow Ball and dinner."

"Dinner I can miss. These thighs aren't getting any thinner." She patted the sides of her slender legs. "And all the damn fudge and cookies this time of year."

He gazed on her orange outline remembering the words to some song he'd heard somewhere—*half woman, half child, she...la, la something...wild.* Didn't sound like elevator music.

"You aren't overweight."

"Your opinion." She sucked in her tummy.

"That's not a healthy attitude." He played with his too-short beard.

"You *are* a shrink, aren't you?"

"What if I am?"

"Spare me." She waved him off like a gnat.

He narrowed his eyes. His shoulders tensed. "What does that mean?"

"You're uptight, kind of paranoid, for a head doctor."

"My days are filled with paranoia." And she'd done it again. Distracting him when she needed…something. What did she want from him? Everyone wanted something.

She hiked up her dress and sat on the carpeted floor.

He looked down and decided she was out of place in this building. Had she been visiting a parent who worked for the Foundation? "What are you doing here?"

"I…I sort of work here at the Le Mare Foundation." Patting the carpet beside her, she motioned for him to sit. "My name is Marie Louise…Smith."

"Work at Le Mare? You can't be more than eighteen." He sat across from her, stared at her freckles, and thought how all young people wanted to be older. Foolishness.

"I'm twenty-three!"

"Sorry." He always had trouble once they were past nine.

"Anyway, I work at Le Mare as part of a…an extracurricular program for my…studies…at the U. They don't pay much, but the perks are great. Maybe I should ask for a raise, you think?"

"Depends. Are you in the psychiatric division?" He glanced at the watch on her wrist. His whole master plan, his entrance into the ball, was going to be ruined.

"No. Probably why we haven't met before."

He didn't answer but rose and paced back and forth a few steps.

"So enough about me. What's your name?"

"Claus."

"Claus. Is that German?"

"Claus is my last name." He scanned the ceiling. Maybe the trap door was disguised. "My first name is Nicholas."

"Well, Nick, I suppose you want me to call you Dr. Claus, but I'm not going to do it. You're stuffy enough without my adding to it. You're just plain ol' Nick to me. Ol' Nick-stuck-in-the-elevator with me."

She could call him whatever she liked. Eventually she'd get around to what she wanted, then she'd use his name properly.

"Oh, my God!" Marie jumped up. "Fall Out Boy." She waved overhead at the speakers. "Fall Out Boy as elevator music. Fall Out Boy singing Christmas music! Is nothing sacred? Now I *am* manic." Her eyes blinked madly.

He wanted to keep his mind on the miracle he needed, but her apparent agitation, and the fact he didn't know Fall Out Boy, distracted him.

"I ask you, Nick. Where is the line drawn? When will the selling out stop? I can't take this!" She raised her hands above her head and plunged them into her hair. Streams of shiny strands covered her fingers like black satin ribbon entwining each digit.

As he took hold of her wrists, he spoke in his calmest singsong voice. "It's all right, Marie Louise. The song will end, and you won't have to listen. Talk to me, and you won't hear the music."

She glanced wildly side-to-side, then moved her head in tiny jerks like an old silent movie; she brought her face to meet his gaze. A soft giggle escaped her mouth. "Or we could just dance. You do dance, don't you, Nick?"

Knowing she'd duped him, he let go. "You're obnoxious. You know that?"

"And you're a tight-ass. Are we even?"

He thought on that for a minute. "I am *not* a tight-ass."

"You are. I'm very intuitive about people." She waved her delicate hand. "And realistic. I see others as clearly as I see myself."

He met her defiant gaze. She had lovely eyes. "How do you see yourself?"

"Don't start that psychology stuff on me." She sat on the floor again, half-smile and half-smirk on her face.

This time he sat next to her. "No psychology, just interest." And he meant it. You had to be interested to actually give people what they needed.

She tilted her head with a sideways glance. "Number one. It's a problem looking eighteen and being twenty-three. It greatly affects my self-image."

"Someday, for the better."

"Oh, please."

"Okay, how old do you think I look?" He smiled inside. Now this was fun.

"Well, you look in pretty good shape." She elbowed him and winked.

For some reason, he puffed his chest. He walked every day and used the gym, as meager as it was. Staying fit for that one big night a year was important.

Her gaze roamed his face. "The blond beard hides a lot, but I'd say forty."

"Wrong. And you've affected me more than I did you." But not adversely. It was great fun fooling people. "I'm actually much older."

She rolled her eyes. "Point taken."

He grinned, pleased by her smiling, relaxed attitude. "And I'm a lot of fun. At least, I provide a great deal of fun for others, so that must mean I'm fun."

Her eyes crinkled at the corners, and her tummy jiggled with a giggle like a bowl full of—

The elevator went dark. "Oh, damn!" They spoke in unison and laughed.

"What's the second?" Nicholas asked.

"What?"

"You said number one, looking too young. What's your number two problem, Marie?" Her hesitation was obvious. "Come on. It's dark and no one is here but me."

"I can't trust anyone anymore." Her tone was sullen. "No one tells me the truth. All the people around me are playing parts."

Isn't everyone? "What part are you playing?"

"I'm...not."

"Yes, you are. Just like everyone else." Except for him, of course, although he'd let her believe him a shrink. "I say we both come clean."

"Okay, you first."

He took a deep breath. Maybe those repeated requests for his honesty had sunk in, and he could be upfront with her. In the dark. "I think you're probably nicer than you let on, and not a spoiled brat under that façade."

"Is that what you meant by coming clean?"

"Young lady –"

"I think you're as stuffy as this elevator."

"You *are* a brat." Uncharacteristic for him to be so blunt, but enough was enough. He was as much fun as the next person who'd spent years in the cold, only being needed once a year, keeping all his real gifts bottled up without appreciation. "I've sky dived."

"No. I don't believe it."

"Yes, I have."

She nudged him. Her tiny shoulder was pointy against his forearm. "Tell me more."

Her interest was a light in the dark. "A few years ago, before...never mind." He cleared his throat. "A few years ago, I spent a week in the Rockies, with only what I could carry on my back. I nearly drowned, white-water rafting."

"Oh, my gosh. I would never have guessed."

"I've done a great many daring and dangerous things." Memories flooded in, seeming more real than the present. "Once a year…well, I try to mix it up now and then, although messing up the routine isn't advised, I am told. I have a great many advisors. But they're small people and don't know it." He should tell them that. They'd have to listen. But then, they were always listening. His life of late was more like sitting in this elevator, immobile. No light. Only mellow elevator music.

"Nick—"

"Shh…listen. It's the Rolling Stones. Now that is blasphemous."

Marie giggled. "I love the Stones."

"I got halfway backstage at their concert before security stopped me."

"Nick!" She leaned into him.

He laughed. A real laugh. None of that ho, ho, ho they expected.

"Give me your hand," she demanded.

"My hand?"

"Come on. You can trust me." She leaned into him again, her hand on his arm. "Give me your hand."

Feeling silly, he complied. Without warning, she stood and pulled him with her.

"Let's dance."

"Oh, I don't think—"

"Come on. No one is here to see us." Her laughter was contagious. "We can't even see ourselves."

Chuckling self-consciously, he followed her lead. They held hands. At first awkward, he relaxed and imagined they danced in perfect sync. A subtle breeze brushed his face, her twirling and laughter disturbing the stale elevator air.

"You're a lovely young lady, Marie Louise."

"Oh, sure. In the dark, I'm a real looker." She let go his hands. "I'm realistic. Remember?"

"Whoa. Stop a minute." He stilled. "Now you give me *your* hand." Using her hand as a guide, he placed his fingers on her shoulder and turned her to face where the mirror would reflect them, if it weren't so dark. "Now look closely and tell me you don't see a beautiful young lady."

"I don't see a beautiful young lady. You're only being kind and a little bit crazy."

"I'm hardly ever kind to anyone over the age of nine." Giving, however you could, that was the important thing. "Look at your gorgeous hair—the color of the sky when the moon is hiding on a cold snowy night. I can see it even in the dark. And your eyes are the color of tree bark against a white landscape. Your face has been kissed with tiny little freckles." As he spoke, he imagined wrapping up his words with a big red ribbon. "How can you not see yourself? I don't think you're as realistic as you say you are. You are a lovely, adorable, intelligent, attractive young woman."

"I am?" The words barely whispered, she intoned awe.

"You are from this moment forward."

"Thank you."

A loud ring choked off the sound of her appreciation. The phone call he hoped for—although the miracle he needed wouldn't happen.

"Oh, good grief, Nick. It's the phone."

In harmony, the lights chimed in on the second ring. He turned and fumbled with the half-opened door of the telephone cubby, grabbing the receiver. "Hello. Hello."

"This is security. We're going to get you out of there soon. Are you okay?"

"Yes. Fine."

"Are you alone or does there happen to be a Mrs. Marie Le Mare with you?"

"Mrs. Le Mare? No. Her name *is* Marie, but her last name is Smith."

She covered her mouth in a giggle and shook her head.

"Well, I might have misunderstood. Let me ask her. Is your last name Le Mare?"

Still giggling with both hands to her face she nodded.

"Apparently, her last name is Le Mare. We'll be waiting." He replaced the receiver and spun around. "You lied."

With a whir, the elevator gave a jerk, knocking him off balance. He grabbed the rail.

Her giggles turned into full laughter.

"You're a brat."

"Now, Nick. Don't be angry. If I'd told you my name was Marie Louise Le Mare, you would've treated me differently."

"You're right! I read a lot of newspapers in the workshop while they're making the toys."

"Toys? What are you—"

"You're the young bride. Married a millionaire old enough to be your father."

"And we wouldn't have had near as much fun, if you'd known." Frowning, she tilted her head to the side. "I get tired of being treated like…like…I could break or something. Besides, playing mind games with you was just too tempting." She punched his shoulder and smiled. "And you have to admit, we had fun."

He couldn't admit anything else. He squinted. The overhead lights did the wave through her hair again. "Yes, Marie, we had fun."

Seconds later, the door opened and a short, over-weight man in gray coveralls greeted them. Two men in white coats stood behind him.

"Hey! Hope you folks are okay. Sorry it took so long, Mrs. Le Mare. Your husband said he'll be right down."

The two white coats stepped forward, one holding a hand out to Nicholas. "Well, Harry. Looks like you had an adventure today. Are you feeling okay?"

He recognized them. Too bad they hadn't sent one of his helpers. These two guys wouldn't be fooled. The attendant who'd waited for him after his session had been too busy playing games on his cell. Slipping past him had posed no challenge at all.

"I'm great. But I don't know why you insist on calling me Harry." He ignored the hand offered and stepped between them. "I haven't missed the Snow Ball, have I?"

"No, no." The short one smiled. "The Snow Ball wouldn't be the same without you."

They were nice enough fellows, even if confused about his identity.

He turned to face Marie. Her eyes opened wide, and her lips parted in a question. Before he could say goodbye, a shout rose behind them.

"Marie! Thank God you're okay." A salt-and-pepper-haired man in a well-cut navy suit strode over.

Ah, the rich husband.

Embracing her, he kissed both of her cheeks. "I'll have the whole system checked out before this building closes tonight."

The two white coats tugged on Nicholas's arms. "Come on, Nick. You're missing the annual Christmas party."

Mr. Le Mare hugged his wife even tighter. "Oh, *mon dieu*. Trapped in the elevator with a crazy man. I've been worried sick."

"Jean, please." She glanced at him. Her face said *sorry*.

It didn't matter. The only opinion that mattered came from those who knew you. You could spend years with some people, like his friends in white, and they didn't have a clue. A half hour with another person, and you gained a true friend for life.

Her husband grabbed her arm. "They said he wasn't dangerous, but he's delusional."

"Is that what they call it?" She smiled at Nicholas. "Maybe we should all be a little more delusional."

He'd come so close to his surprise appearance at the Snow Ball, although only a miracle would've made his solo entrance possible. She hadn't needed his help—not the way he first thought—but a gift had been given. And returned in kind.

This was a Christmas miracle he hadn't counted on.

Never Alone on Christmas

A ringing phone at two in the morning never brought good news.

Jonathan Jay Somefun blinked at the orange iridescent numbers on his bedside clock. The phone rang a second time as the digital readout rolled over to 2:01. Still, he didn't move. Last time he got a call at two in the morning, the hospital gave him the news—Lola was gone. Fourth ring. Fifth ring. He couldn't think of anything bad that could be waiting on the other side of the call. His elbow creaked as he stretched to grab the receiver.

"'Lo?"

"Hey, Dad, I wasn't about to hang up. I have an early Christmas present for you."

His oldest son, living in Austria, hadn't allowed for the time difference. "David? Nothing's wrong?" He rubbed his eyes and swung his feet over the edge of the bed.

"No, Dad. Everything's fine. You're a grandpa for the third time. It's a boy!"

"A boy? Ah, that's great, son. How's Annie doing?"

"Great. She sends her love and says Merry Christmas. We wanted you to know that Jonathan Derrick Somefun entered the world tonight."

He opened his mouth in exclamation, but his throat tightened. He swallowed. "Why, son…I'm…well, thanks."

"He's got lots of thick black hair and looks just like his grandpa."

"Let's hope he grows out of that."

David laughed. "I'll let you get back to sleep, Dad. Sure wish we could see you for Christmas." The sound of a scraping chair. His son cleared his throat. "You have someone special to spend it with, don't you?"

"You know I do." Couldn't let him worry. "Give Annie and little…Jonathan a kiss."

"Love you, Dad. Bye."

He set the phone back on the nightstand. *Ain't that something?* Another Jonathan Somefun. He chuckled and settled back into bed. Staring into the dark, the contented feeling subsided as he thought about the call in the night a few years back.

Lola had been a good woman. Her orange hair complemented his dark Choctaw skin when she walked next to him. Her plain face wasn't too wrinkled for a woman nearly sixty. She'd work an extra shift at the hospital now and then, just so she could buy her man fine clothes. His wardrobe had flourished. And for their one Christmas together, she'd given him a gold bracelet. He crossed his arms over his chest, the metal of the jewelry cool on his skin, and the memory of her smile on that morning warm in his heart.

"You're my Jonny Jay, and you should dress like uptown," Lola would tell him. "Las Vegas has never seen such a sight as you. And when you dance, well, I think the Tropicana is going to find out and start a male revue just for you."

He laughed out loud.

In the eight months they had been married, he'd never even looked at another woman. Had no desire to stray. He cared for her kindness, attentiveness, and sweet personality.

Lola just might have been the perfect one.

No one had known Lola had cancer. Not even Lola. Until she'd passed out working the mid shift in the hospital cafeteria. That had been a Wednesday. She'd died on Sunday.

He scrunched deeper under the covers, shrugged his shoulders and head against the pillow, and closed his eyes thinking about his newborn namesake.

A ringing phone could bring good news at two in the morning.

He'd told his son he wouldn't be alone for Christmas. *We'll see.*

****

Jonathan jiggled his drink, clinking the ice cubes as he sat on the same stool he'd posed on the last four nights at the Riverside Casino bar. He glanced toward the stage where the band would play later. A drink and a few turns around the dance floor kept a man's heart in good shape, kept a man's youth from fading entirely.

"So, how's it hangin' tonight, Somefun?" The bartender slid a fresh napkin under Jonathan's glass.

He liked being called Somefun, and he liked the way the bartender paused between some and fun. Women always seemed to call him Jonny, and men usually tagged him JJ.

"Hey, Carl, the night is young, and so am I."

The bartender laughed. "Are you going to hit the dance floor tonight, Somefun? Show these tourists and river rats how?"

"Damn straight!" He offered a wide grin. "That is, if there's any decent looking women in the house tonight."

Carl leaned his elbows on the bar. "Just how decent does she have to be?"

"Not *that* decent."

He found it easy conversing with bartenders. As an underage, Native American kid bar hopping in Los Angeles, engaging the barkeeps had been necessary so they didn't question his ethnicity. In the '50s, there had still been some bars that refused to sell whiskey to American Indians. So, Somefun had become Ramirez, passing himself off as a smooth-talking Mexican-American. He still carried his fake I. D. pressed between his Social Security card and a picture of his sons when they were four and five.

A woman in her twenties slid onto the stool one over and ordered a Margarita. Carl gave him a wink. He considered moving closer, but only for an instant. He took in the long, blonde hair pulled back in a pink ribbon, slim arms, and clean-scrubbed face. He smelled the scent of lemons through the smoke of the casino. Way too young, he judged. Seventy-six years of experience and his cosmopolitan point of view would overwhelm her.

Jonathan Jay Somefun needs a mature, worldly woman. And maybe this time, one a little tired of seeing the world. The past year with Josephine had worn him down. He hadn't admitted it at the time. For the sake of his waistline, he cut back on the booze and needed a few more hours of beauty sleep each night. He'd called it his new style, but Josephine had just called him old. He hadn't cheated on her either. His new style had changed that pattern. But after six months, the dew was off the pumpkin. Josephine was no spring chicky. Her makeup reminded him of war paint. And when she'd gone on the warpath, he'd loaded up two suitcases of new clothes and four pairs of leather shoes. The year hadn't been a total loss. But trying to get over Lola with the likes of Josephine hadn't been one of his finer moments.

It had been time to leave Los Angeles anyway. The atmosphere had sapped his vitality like a leech sucking on blood-starved muscles.

The blonde didn't look his way, picked up her drink, and headed for the dance floor.

"Need another one?" Carl nodded at his half-empty glass.

"Nah. Not yet." He gazed out the window behind the bar. The lights from both banks of the river reflected on the black surface in wavy gyrations.

It was a good move, coming to Bullhead City, Arizona, a town with dry, clean air, stretching sinuously alongside the Colorado River. The casinos of Laughlin littered the banks on the Nevada side. During the day, the barren, rocky shoreline was alive with pleasure boaters and jet-skiers sunning or parking to migrate into the casinos. After the sun burned out, the lights of the gambling houses set the river on fire. Dropping cash at the tables gave them a buzz the fast craft couldn't supply.

"Hey, Carl, I ever tell you about my boys? David is a minister, and Larry is a lawyer. Raised 'em myself." His chest puffed with pride whenever he spoke of his children. "I'm a granddad three times over."

"Which wife you stay with long enough to get you two kids?"

"Ruby, my first one."

Carl set two beers on the counter and popped the lids. "How many wives you had, Somefun?"

"Only three. Not so many."

The bartender stepped away, handed off the beers, and returned. "And how many women you had?"

"Now, Carl, I ain't one to kiss and tell, but there's been a sight more of those. And I reckon a few more to go." He raised his glass in a toast and took a drink.

Carl laughed. "So you left L. A. lookin' for that next Mrs. Somefun? That one particular beauty?"

"Arizona, L. A., or Timbuktu—they're *all* beauties."

The bartender glanced up and down the bar. When no new customers presented themselves, he leaned on his elbows in front of Jonathan. "Ruby in L. A. and, I think you said, Lola in Las Vegas was your third wife. Who and where did number two strike?"

He stared into his glass and sighed. "Might not have been a number three, if I'd been a wiser man." But then he wouldn't have met Lola, and that would've been a shame. "Ethel was a handsome woman."

Since she was moneyed from a previous marriage, and since his sons were on their own, he'd been able to assume the role he'd chosen as a no-responsibilities, female-loving kind of guy. Finding the financial means to enjoy his idea of retirement had been the dilemma until he'd found Ethel. In wife number two, with her love of fun and a seemingly endless supply of money, he'd found his means.

"Ethel stood nearly six feet tall, and in our stocking feet, we met eye to eye." Her girth was almost too much for him to get his arms around, but she was strong and nimble, which relieved him of any real work around the house. "She was a beauty that favored bright colored dresses and layers of jewelry."

"Sounds like you strayed from the golden goose."

"That I did." He considered the unflattering characterization the bartender coined. *True that.* "And I got what I deserved. A cocktail waitress at the Palomino Club turned my head one night. If my hand hadn't been where it was and one of Ethel's friends hadn't seen me and blabbed…well, I might still be married." He shrugged. That little gal was so sweet and firmer than anything he'd had since he was eighteen. He remembered thinking she'd probably be the last young thing he'd ever touch again.

"A lesson learned, Carl. A man has to know his limitations and embrace his age at some point in life." He was damn good with the women, but he wasn't getting any younger. About time he got wiser. "I married her for all the wrong reasons. Gotta say, Carl, the woman deserved better."

Marriage number two ended with Ethel's quietly spoken words.

"Jonny, you're a no good, two-timing, drunk. It's no wonder your first wife ended up in the nut house. It's beyond me how you raised two boys to be such good human beings when you're so loathsome. Now get out of my house."

Yep, lesson learned. Then he'd met Lola. And damned if his new style couldn't have seen him through the rest of his life…if she hadn't died. He missed her sweet smile and warm heart. Yep, she'd been the one to settle down with. Maybe her being yanked away from him was some kind of punishment. That Karma stuff…if you believed in that.

"Hey, barkeep. Can I get a vodka tonic?" a voice called out from the end of the bar. Carl tapped the wood, nodded, and shuffled away.

Multi-colored lights suddenly blinked around the edge of the bar, and in a corner by the stage a Christmas tree came to life. "Looks like the holidays have come to Laughlin." His chest went hollow. He chided himself. It wasn't possible to get to the boys this year, but he'd damn well find a way to celebrate.

He hated spending Christmas alone.

Jonathan heard the music in the lounge start up. As his white patent leather shoes touched the floor, he two-stepped out of the bar and over to the adjoining lounge. Standing behind the brass rail separating the lounge from the casino, he flexed his biceps under the snug fitting, shiny polyester shirt and tapped his right foot to the music. The four-piece band played standard pop tunes from the past five decades. Jonathan watched the couples moving back and forth, up and down, no one touching, no one twirling.

I need to show these people how it's done. He'd had the same thought every night for a week, and although he managed two dances three nights ago, the clientele during the week consisted mostly of retired couples and newlyweds. Tonight, Friday night, would bring in the local ladies and the people up from Phoenix.

The band launched into a fifties rock and roll tune. He stepped into the lounge and approached a table of four women. They appeared to be two sets of mothers and daughters.

"Would any of you lovely ladies care to jitterbug?"

The dark-haired mother on his right smiled. "I can do that."

He took her hand. The wedding ring pressed into his palm as he led her to the middle of the square dance floor. This would be a one-dance lady. He started with a simple step until he judged her ability as fair, then led her into a sideways maneuver and a twirl. She was tight and a touch off beat, but he managed to turn it into a pretty fair display.

He scanned the tables as they danced around his arena until two women sitting next to the Christmas tree caught his eye. He had their full attention. Jonathan smiled and dipped, keeping the beat and rhythm of his moves at pace with the fast music. While everyone around the couple bobbed up and down in solitary fashion, he and his partner moved through in harmony.

When the song ended, he bent slightly forward, knees locked in a gallant bow. "Thank you, lovely lady."

After escorting her back to her friends, he strolled across the dance floor to the two women bathed in the lights from the tree. "Good evening, ladies. I couldn't help but notice you sitting here and hoped you might allow me to buy you a drink."

"Only if you'll sit and have one with us." The thin brunette with a wide smile and a long face spoke up.

"I would be most honored. My name is Jonathan Jay

Somefun."

"Well Jonny, ain't that the truth." A high pitch giggle erupted. "My name is Adele, and this here's Mae. We sure did enjoy your dancing." She batted lashes over narrow-set eyes.

He tipped his head in thanks, glanced at Mae, and met her pale blue gaze with a smile. He judged both women to be near sixty, no wedding rings, and not tourists. Mae was short, a little round in a matronly way, with cropped silver-white hair that sparkled with the tree lights. She had a close-mouthed smile and eyes that saw beyond his polyester shirt. The band began their rendition of "Money for Nothing."

With his gaze still on Mae, he asked, "Do you ladies dance?"

They both spoke at once. Adele gushed, "Oh no, Jonny, not like that!" While Mae answered quietly, "As a matter of fact, I do, Jonathan."

The use of his full name, her quiet reply, and steady gaze dimmed the surroundings. She had his full attention. "Well, then, this song sounds like a good one. May I have the pleasure?" He dipped his head and held out a hand. "Adele, do you mind? Maybe you could catch the cocktail waitress for our drinks?"

He sensed the confidence in Mae's step and didn't hold back as the jitterbug began. She followed with grace and rhythm. The fast song led right into a slow one, an old Johnny Mathis song, "When I Fall in Love." Since Mae gave no indication of wanting to return to the table, he pulled her respectfully closer.

With a deep breath of her lilac scent, he cocked his head at an angle to address her. "Mae, you are a fine dancer. I can't tell you how much I enjoy dancing with an attractive woman who knows her way around the dance floor."

She murmured a quiet thank you.

"Do you live around here?"

She nodded. "In Bullhead."

"What do you know? So do I. Just moved here a couple of weeks ago. How 'bout you?"

"I've lived here for five years. After my husband died, I decided to retire here." She glanced toward her friend. "I knew Adele and her daughter, so it was easy."

He lowered his voice, expressing true sympathy, yet flushed happily with the news. "I'm sorry to hear about your husband. Were you married long?"

"Thank you, Jonathan." Her sweet smile returned. "Oh yes, thirty-five years."

"Well, isn't that wonderful." He pressed his fingers gently into her back. "Marriage is a great and honorable thing. Although I am currently single, I much prefer the married life myself."

"Do you?" Her smile widened. "I guess I would say so, too. I've been having quite a time living close to all this nightlife. Although after a while, every night is a little bit the same." She batted her eyelids and dipped her chin before gazing into his face again. "But I thought you would be more the partying type."

"Now Mae, why would you say that?"

"Well, Jonathan, you dance so beautifully and seem to have a way about yourself."

"And you, too, dance beautifully, and I've seen the men looking at you."

Mae was artfully flattered and held her head a notch higher as he smiled down on her.

The dance ended, and as they stepped back from each other, still holding hands, a disco song from the '70s began. He twirled her twice, and they danced once more, Jonathan lavishing the compliments all the while, before returning to the table and a bored looking Adele.

"I was thinking about leaving, Mae." Adele's voice was flat.

"Oh, Adele, it isn't so late yet." Mae's brow wrinkled, and she clasped her hands to her chest.

His hopes rose. "Now Mae, if Adele would prefer to go, I would be happy to see you safely home. I have my car parked on the other side of the river. If you don't mind riding the ferry boat across, I could see you to your door."

The long-faced woman frowned an obvious "don't do it" expression.

But Mae didn't hesitate. "Thank you, Jonathan. I wouldn't mind a ferry boat ride."

Her friend pushed her chair back from the table and glared. "I'll leave, but it's not a good idea. I want you to call me when you get home." With a huff, she stomped away.

His new companion's cheeks pinked. "I'm sorry, Jonathan. Adele surely has a vivid imagination. She really is a nice person."

It was nothing new to him. Choosing one female at a table over another, leaving one scorned, was a way of life. He was lucky to be rid of Adele so quickly. There was a time when he could've played this scene out for several hours and not whittle it down to one woman until an hour before last call for alcohol. But those were days gone by, and the nights seemed shorter now. It wasn't that his pace was any slower than it used to be; he preferred a different style now. That's what it was, merely his new style.

Besides, he had a feeling about Mae.

Another hour of dancing and talking. He learned Mae lived comfortably by herself. One son lived in Michigan. She'd seen many a fun time with her husband. Now, she enjoyed the heat, the river, an occasional night at the casino, and she'd forgotten how much she loved to dance. He listened until nearing ten o'clock.

"I've really enjoyed myself, but I need to get home and let out my dog." He could hear the love she had for the animal in her voice.

"What kind of dog?"

"Puddin' is a Chihuahua."

"Chihuahuas are my favorite dog," Jonathan told her, not entirely dishonest. He'd never considered what kind of dog he liked. But if Mae liked them, he could, too.

They rode the boat from Nevada to the Arizona side. The air was dry, tinged with the scent of fish, and cool. As they ferried across, Jonathan didn't miss the opportunity to tell Mae how she shone in the moonlight. In fact, the moonlight paled in comparison. And he meant it. By the time he'd driven her to her door, Mae expressed he come in for a moment and meet Puddin'. And when they realized it was eleven o'clock and watching the reruns of Jeopardy was a nightly habit they had in common, another half an hour passed pleasantly. Plans were made for the following evening, and he kissed her gently on the cheek.

※※※※

Most evenings they sat on her patio and watched the sun extinguish itself as it washed red and orange over the mountains, glistening in the Colorado River, until the final embers settled in hues of smoky purple. The sparkling river twinkled brighter than his diamond cufflinks. He found the richness of the desert colors more gratifying than the nightlights he'd chased for so many years.

"Mae." He took her hand one evening as they gazed across the river. Puddin' lounged in his lap and licked their entwined fingers resting on his thigh. "You're a precious woman."

"I do enjoy your company, Jonathan. But…"

His heart pinched. Had he found his forever only to

have it yanked from his grasp? He didn't want to lose her. Didn't want any more nights standing at the railing and hoping to meet a woman who wanted to meet him. Had he misread the sweetness Mae showered on him? Had she just been biding her time until…what?

Her pale blue eyes blinked as she appeared to search for the right words. "I know you're a worldly man, and from what we've told each other about our pasts, you require variety in your life, whereas I'm satisfied with my quiet existence here. I treasure each day now, and although you and I may only share a short time—"

"Are you ill?"

"Ill? No. Why do you ask?"

"It sounded like…never mind." He squeezed her hand as his heart returned to normal. "I treasure you." The thought of living without Mae, the river, and the desert chilled his arms as if the last rays of the sun refused to warm him. "I might've seen a bit more of the world than you have. But I've seen more in these last few weeks than the seventy decades before you showed me. "I'm happy, Mae. I hoped you were, too."

Puddin' gave his fingers one last lick and buried his nose in the fold of Jonathan's slacks.

"You won't get bored? With me? With us?"

He'd always had a golden tongue and a way with the ladies. But glib conversation escaped him. This moment required more. He brought her fingers to his lips and brushed them with a kiss. "No." Emotion in his throat joked the one word. "No, sweet Mae."

Three days before Christmas, Jonathan moved in with Mae. He found his new style of living fit him better than the two dozen polyester shirts and leather dancing shoes taking up more than half of Mae's closet.

He sold the gold bracelet from Lola to buy Christmas

gifts for the dog and Mae. He was sure Lola would approve—wouldn't want him to spend the rest of his life alone. Jonathan beamed with the new life he'd found when he opened his gift of a coffee mug that said "Puddin's Papa" on their first Christmas.

Twice a week they rode the ferry across the Colorado River and ate dinner at the Riverside Casino, dancing afterwards until it was time to go home and let out their furry friend.

Jonathan couldn't think of a chapter in his life that was happier…except maybe the births of his sons. But deep in his heart, he recognized he'd reached the last chapter.

And Puddin's Papa was never alone on Christmas again.

Love in the Vault

This was the absolute last time she'd kiss anyone under the mistletoe. A dozen red flags and ringing alarms should've sounded when Harold King nudged her under the poisonous berries.

The guy had never paid her the time of day before. Between the wine punch and his cobalt blue eyes, her head went all woozy and blocked all logical thoughts, obscuring suspicions. *But wow.* Eleanor licked her lips. The kiss was close to perfect, other than the vodka fumes…until he whispered in her ear, "This really is my gun, although I'm very glad to see you."

Getting kissed under what should've been strictly Christmas decoration, by a man she'd desired from afar, had her so addled she allowed him to lead her to the elevator. When he drew the gun and nudged her forward, she decided this must be some kind of a joke perpetrated by her friend, Cricket. Harold snugged close to her back in the confines of the elevator, the gun poking her in the ribs while his other hand clasped her shoulder. She scanned the crowded room searching for a laughing Cricket before the doors closed and trapped her.

The joke had gone too far. The lump in her throat grew, and confusion spun her head. This *must* be a joke. "Did Cricket put you up this?" Yet, in the quiet closeness, the elevator plummeted along with her clenched stomach, tight lungs, and shaky legs. "That's a toy gun, right?" She squirmed to turn around, but his fingers pinched into her shoulders.

"I don't play with toys." He flicked the gun in front of her face long enough for the light overhead to reflect on the metal, then back to her ribs. "Ah, Eleanor, Head of Accounting. You keep your nose in the numbers too much." He made a clicking noise. "You really are a bit dense, aren't you?"

"That's not nice." His remark stung almost as bad as having a gun held against her.

After all, he was the third highest ranking executive, not to mention the second best-looking man in the company. A gun. *Damn Cricket*. Real gun made the joke more real, right? She relaxed slightly with the thought. Cricket chose Harold for the swoon factor, which was just mean. Some best friend. Although she did get a kiss. A quiver managed to sneak in around the insult. "I'm not den—"

"Think about it, hon. I got fired today for company disloyalty. Hmm…why would I be pissed off?"

"You got fired?" She craned her head to peer over her shoulder and into his face. "For disloyalty?"

"See, Eleanor? That's what I mean. You really ought to look up from your computer once in a while."

Criminy. She'd heard rumblings, and the books told her Harold King wasn't worth the number of zeroes on his check. But why didn't she know he'd been fired? "What do you want, Harold? I think this has gone on quite long enough. Why are you doing this?" She stared at his face reflected in the mirrored walls.

"Oh, don't look so surprised. It was five minutes to five when that son of a bitch Cline got the nerve to drop the bomb. You're probably not the only one left out of the loop." The gun poked around her ribs while he fidgeted in anger. He brought it to rest against her side. "Cline, the mealy wimp, called Roman in for back up. Meathead and brawn combined to give me the ax. The son of a bitch thinks he can just ruin me like this?" Harold's face went hard, his teeth grinding.

Eleanor's heart skipped a beat as she glanced down at the metal nestled against her side. *This is no joke.* "What have I got to do with this?"

The melodic chime of the elevator signaled the basement level, and the door swooshed open. No Christmas decorations down here. The vault, shelving, records…no one to see or hear them. She curled her toes inside her black pumps, gripping the soles, throwing weight to her heels, and plastering her feet to the floor of the elevator.

"Please, Harold. I didn't have anything to do with your dismissal."

"My dismissal? You make it sound so innocuous." With a heavy hand on her shoulder, he whipped her around to face him, shoving her against the mirrored elevator wall and transferring the weapon's barrel to the soft spot below her breastbone. "You're always so in control, aren't you?"

Her heart clamored. Her knees weakened. The familiar, dark-lashed eyes, which usually gave her goosebumps, glowered like a Halloween ghoul. Oh, damn the mistletoe and damn her fantasies. "Wh…what are you going to do?"

He leaned in, only the gun separating their bodies.

Would he take his anger out on her?

He cocked his head and stared into her eyes, so close his breath flowed over her face and slithered onto her bare collarbone. The restricting hand on her shoulder lifted, slipped to the back of her head, and pulled out the comb holding the hair off her neck. "I've thought about getting this close to you now and then."

She'd thought about it *more* than now and then. Only Roman, Jack Roman, played the role more often in her dreams than Harold. Jack, the best-looking man in the company. In the world. Roman, Jack Roman held the same level of sensuality as Bond, James Bond when it came to weaving fantasies. A knee leaned heavily against her thigh, effectively disrupting her digression. "Why…would…you…notice me?"

"Your ass. You have a great ass, Eleanor. One thing Roman and I agree on."

"Ro…Roman?" Jack *had* noticed her. Even though the thought of them discussing her ass creeped her out.

"Hmmm. Yeah, nice ass. And with your hair down…" He tilted his head and studied her face.

Oh hell. The knee slipped between her legs. She couldn't breathe. He was going to act out some warped fantasy before leaving the company. "With…a…gun?" Her voice croaked, not sounding like herself at all.

"What?"

Her lip trembled. "Did your conjecture include a gun?"

"See?" He pulled away, jerked her from the wall, and resumed the gun in the back position. "You think too much. Exactly the reason why you head home alone every night."

How rude. Despite her fear, anger welled. Why ever did she find this man attractive? She'd never been drawn to bad boys. But then, he'd never shown this side around the office.

"Now get your cute little ass out of the elevator." He shoved.

She reared back. "I didn't get you fired. Don't take your anger out on me. I've always been nice—"

"Shut up, Eleanor."

This time, he shoved with force, the gun so sharp between her back ribs she cried out.

"Keep moving."

The slick soles of her black leather pumps slid over the mud-brown vinyl of the basement floor as he manhandled her forward. An exhaust fan clicked on overhead but didn't relieve the stuffy confines of the windowless, cement-walled tomb. She gave a quick glance back as her only escape, the elevator, disappeared when he manipulated her beyond the shelving.

He yanked her around the bank of file cabinets and nudged her toward the vault.

The vault.

Eleanor gasped. Harold wasn't looking for a quiet corner to pick up where they'd left off under the mistletoe. He wanted access to the vault.

A vision of being locked away in the mammoth safe for the weekend, no water, no food, and no bathroom brought renewed trembling to her knees. Pretending to stumble was easy as she lurched forward and grabbed at a handle on the last cabinet. With her other hand, she clutched the edge of the metal drawers and whirled to face him, putting the corner of the cabinet between them and the gun in her gut. He wouldn't just take the money and let her go. For some reason, she felt certain he wasn't a murderer. He wouldn't shoot her. But she'd be locked up until Mr. Cline came for the funds to make Monday's deposit. Because, unfortunately, Harold pegged her correctly. She did always go home alone. Who'd notice she'd left the party?

"Please, please reconsider what you're doing."

"What do you think I'm doing, Eleanor with the sweet ass?" Pulling her away from the filing cabinet, he drew her close.

"Money." She gulped. His grasp wasn't exactly rough, more like the hunk taking possession of the bare-chested beauty on the cover of an old-fashioned romance novel. She always did find those covers revolting. "You're…you are after the money, right?"

"Mmm...yes, that's what I'm after, but maybe you'd like to share in the wealth. I've seen you looking at me—with less than pure thoughts." His midnight-blue eyes were partially veiled by thick lashes. The effect, meant to be purely sensual, sent shivers of another variety.

Her neck burned hot while her mouth went dry.

"I could be your Santa, baby. Put a little something in your stockings. Actually, it would be anything but little."

"Oh," she gasped, sure her face now glowed with red hot heat. "That's just disrespectfully rude."

His laugh rumbled deep. "Joking, Eleanor. Although, under better circumstances, I wouldn't mind finding out how your sweet ass looks in a string bikini. But you're not a likely companion for an escape to a faraway beach with a suitcase full of stolen goods."

"You're not the least bit funny." Her attempted bravado was met with a smirk.

He released her, reached between the last two filing cabinets, and brought out a canvas bag the size of a small suitcase.

"It won't work. Two people are required to enter the code." Maybe he didn't know she could open the vault alone. "Let me go, and I'll forget this ever happened."

"Any combination of you, Roman, and Cline, right?" His sneer erased her hope for an out. "But there's one bewitching hour a day when any one of you can unlock the door. You give me about as much credit as our asshole boss allots me." He spun her around, forcing her to take the last few steps to the vault. "Okay, let's get this business concluded. The magic hour is ticking away, and I have a plane waiting."

"Is a few thousand really worth the risk? You could go to prison for a very long time."

"A few thousand?" The sneer in his voice meant he knew more about the accounting than she'd hoped.

"Yes, you know most customers don't deal in cash." She continued her bluff, holding a glimmer of hope that he had only a vague idea of what the vault could hold in the company's busiest month of the year.

"Nice try, babe. I'm guessing you don't know the half of it." He leaned his face close to her ear. "Fun and games are over. Open it. *Now*." His growl sent shivers down her spine.

She had no idea what he meant, but the time had come to quit stalling. With a shaky hand, she tapped the code into the digital lock. The click punched the quiet, stuffy air, signaling the release.

Harold dragged Eleanor into the vault. "Have a seat, sweet ass." He nudged her onto the L-shaped, leather bench to her right.

She collapsed into the corner, facing toward the far wall.

"I think you're going to enjoy the show. My guess is you haven't spent much time in Cline's safe."

"You have?"

"Not physically. Although, I was privy to the original *general plans* for the company." He set the canvas on the table in the center of the room, unbuckled the leather straps, and unzipped the bag. "Cline and I go way back. To college. He knew he'd take over the business from his father and run it differently than old Dad. I was with him from the beginning. Then he got greedy. He decided he needed another man to be his second—someone who didn't know as much about his roots."

Roman, Jack Roman.

He withdrew two lengths of rope from the bag.

"Oh." Tied up. Left in the vault? Oh god, she'd die. "Please, Harold. I won't move. You don't need to tie me up."

"Put your hands behind your back."

"Harold—"

He stuck the gun in her face. "I'm really serious here. If you're lucky, I won't kill you, but how would you like a bullet somewhere that would incapacitate you? I can't have you getting a sudden brave urge to stop me." He brought his face close to hers. "I see a little hint of rebellion in those pretty hazel eyes of yours."

Her heart hammered, and she swallowed deep. Wordlessly, she clasped her hands behind her back and rotated her shoulders, giving him access to her wrists.

"That's a good girl." With one hand, Harold gripped Eleanor's wrists while he pivoted enough to set the gun on the table. After wrapping her wrists in rope, he knelt in front of her and did the same with her ankles.

She held her breath as his hands manipulated her legs and feet, but he seemed intent solely on subduing her and getting back to the robbery.

"What you don't know about is the part of the business Cline conducts on his own." Harold stood next to the table surveying their tight surroundings.

The vault was the size of a roomy walk-in closet. The table could double for a freestanding butcher block in a kitchen. The L-shaped bench she sat on shared the walls with the door and the other wall to her right along with two ancient, wooden, filing cabinets. Cardboard boxes that looked as if they dated back as far as the filing cabinets and a three-foot-by-three-foot portrait of a man who looked like Mr. Cline occupied the wall to the left of the door. The fourth wall was shelving with various sizes of the type of metal boxes found in bank safety deposit boxes.

Harold moved to the shelves. "The jackass is going to feel a pinch come Monday." His muttered remark seemed to be made to himself. He started pulling boxes, peeking inside, and either returning them or setting them on the wooden table. Three large and one smaller one met his approval.

Eleanor leaned against the wall with her shoulders, wiggled her fingers for circulation, and attempted to even her breathing. As Harold opened the first box and transferred banded currency to the canvas bag, she swore she heard a quiet swooshing noise. Straining her ears for any sounds outside the safe, she held her breath. Someone to rescue her? Foolish. A fantasy.

When her captor opened the second bank box and transferred more banded bills to his bag, she sat up straighter. The quiet gasp that escaped caught his attention.

"Oh, yes. I told you, your boss has a lot more going than you or anyone else knows about." He shoved the second container aside and emptied the third. "I left the fourth one full. And the one with the checks, of course. After all, he'll need to make his deposit on Monday." He laughed. "But the best is yet to come." Lifting the small box in a movement to dump the contents into the canvas, he paused. "You should see this." He removed what looked like several plastic sandwich bags and stepped in front of her. With his fingers spread, palms up, the bags made a jumbled display of sparkling glass pieces.

"Are those...?" She swallowed, mesmerized by the colors and sizes.

"Precious, aren't they? Diamonds, rubies, emeralds." He clutched them all together and whipped around, leaving her with her mouth gaping open. "Just a little side business to compliment the legal, respectable jewelry company left to him by dear old Dad." He nodded at the portrait on the wall. "The beauty of this theft is it'll go unreported. The money and checks I've left behind are considerable, certainly enough for the biggest month of the year. And this." He thumped the side of the bag. "This is unrecorded, mostly illegal, and would expose Cline and possibly his more *discreet* customers." He shrugged his shoulders and grinned his once charming, but now smarmy, smile. "Looks like it might be tough to make the yacht payment this month."

Eleanor's mind reeled. Mr. Cline certainly wasn't what he seemed.

Harold zipped the bag.

Panic rose in her throat.

He lifted the canvas bag with both hands. "My just severance and holiday bonus. Merry Christmas, Harold King."

As she opened her mouth to beg him not to leave her in this tomb, something sounded outside the vault. She froze. Nothing. Maybe it was the pulse of fear pounding in her head. Harold didn't seem to notice. There. Again. Not really a sound, but…intuition? Someone else's presence.

"Drop the bag." Jack Roman's command sent her heart to her throat.

But Harold was quick. He let go of the money and snatched the gun in a fluid movement, whirling to face Jack standing in the doorway. "Well, well, if it isn't the brawn of the company, coming to save the day." His face hardened. "Back off, Roman."

The air left Eleanor's lungs. She thought she might faint. Jack would win in an even confrontation, but not against a gun. Oh gawd, would Harold shoot him?

Jack flicked what looked like a wink. *Really, Eleanor! Now is not the time for wishful thinking.*

"I can't let you walk away, can I, King?"

"You don't have a choice, unless you'd like to see how handy I am with my equalizer."

Jack's eyes narrowed as he seemed to consider his options. "Let Eleanor go, and we'll address the situation."

"You always did have a good sense of humor, Roman."

He reached behind him and with effort hefted the canvas from the table, the gun not wavering from his co-worker's chest. "Have a seat. You can cozy up to little miss sweet ass." His knuckles whitened with the grip on the gun. "It's not a request." He dipped his aim to Jack's crotch. "I don't have any qualms about maiming you, if you don't do as I say."

Jack's full lips quirked upward as he lowered onto the bench beside her, coming into contact from shoulder to knee. "Are you okay?" His gaze followed the gun, but his quiet question floated over her.

"Yes." She could've scooted away, given him room, but she relaxed with the weight of his warmth and strength against her.

"Hey, you two look good together. Too bad there isn't any mistletoe overhead." Harold snickered as he paused in the doorway. "Goodbye. And I do mean goodbye. Oh, and Merry Christmas." He backed out, the gun disappearing last.

Eleanor tensed, waiting for Jack to make his lunge. Surely he'd stop Harold from locking them in the vault. There must be something he could do. *Do something, Roman, Jack Roman!*

The heavy whoosh of the door and then the click of the lock caused every muscle in her body to collapse with defeat, and she slumped against the wall. "Oh, no," she whimpered.

Jack's arm slipped behind her. "Here. Sit forward a little. Let me get you untied."

"What are we going to do?"

He pulled the rope from her hands.

"How can we possibly spend the whole weekend in here?" She massaged her wrists then wrung her fingers as she glanced around their prison. When he didn't answer, she tipped her head to look into his face. The slight smile that usually undid her curved his mouth. *First, he makes no effort to overtake Harold, and now all he can do is smile? Some brawn.*

He pushed the hair from her face, his fingers gliding over her cheek. "It'll be okay."

A shaky breath and the tentacles of fear closing around her chest neutralized the electric sensation of what seemed like a caress. "Okay?" But she'd had enough for one day of so-called high-powered executives fooling her. She flicked the hair from the other side of her face before he could repeat the action. Even in the presence of the most gorgeous man in the company, the tight space and an obvious lack of air tightened her throat with panic. And all he could do was coo and smile. Anger simmered.

"Let me get your feet free." Jack knelt in front of Eleanor, quickly releasing the rope from her ankles. When he stood, he offered his hand.

She pinched her lips and stood without his help, prancing away and around to the side of the table. When she pivoted in a huff, prepared to question his lack of bravado in the face of their impending doom, the sight of his relaxed stance and teasing expression froze her intentions.

Dove gray eyes regarded her, crinkled at the corners as if amused. His smile was a flirtation when his bottom lip twitched. Both hands were tucked in his pants pockets, his head tilted just so. She hadn't noticed before that he was without his tie, and his jacket hung unbuttoned. Although covered in a shirt and jacket, his biceps bulged, challenging the restraint of material. The open shirt collar exposed his strong neck and a hint of a well-formed chest. She couldn't stop herself from gazing down the line of shirt buttons and imagining tight abs beneath the pale green material.

He cleared his throat.

She startled.

"I know I've never said so, but you have lovely hair."

Her hand went involuntarily to push the tresses off her neck. The compliment left her speechless…but only momentarily. "I can't believe you're talking about my hair when we could be hours from suffocating in this tomb."

"We're fine. Maybe—"

"Fine?" She stomped within inches of him. Someone needed to take control of this disaster. "How the hell can you be so blasé about our situation? Why did you let that bozo escape and lock us in here? Why didn't you—"

"I was going to say, maybe I should explain." He'd taken her by the shoulders, and his thumbs resting on the bare skin where the dress ended below her collarbone did more to rob her of speech than his interruption. "All right?"

She stepped back from his seemingly innocent embrace, merely nodding.

A frown passed over his face. "I'm sorry."

His touch had weakened her resolve, but she clung to the control her anger had lent. She waved a hand through the air. "Continue."

"I saw King kiss you. It struck me as odd. Not odd that he'd want to kiss you." He shuffled his feet. "But what he was doing at the party, after having been fired. I wondered if there was something…between you. I didn't think there could be. The man's a dolt, and you're…" He studied her face.

She hitched a small gasp. The anger fled in a whoosh. The goosebumps his words caused sent little jolts of fire from her shoulders to her toes. "What, Jack? What am I?"

"You're so much more than he deserves." He swallowed, inhaled deeply, and continued. "When I saw you in the elevator, the way you stood, and the expression on your face, I thought something was wrong, and I had to follow. I took the stairs and reached the first floor before you did. When the elevator continued to the basement, I was certain something was wrong."

The concern on his face furrowed his brow. She wanted

to hug him, throw herself into his arms, and bury her face in his chest.

"The stairs are at the other end of the basement from the elevator, and by the time I crept to within sight of you and King, you were headed into the vault with a gun at your back. That's when I headed back upstairs."

Like a shot of cold water, the warm fuzzies were washed away, and she jerked. "You what?"

"I recognized the gun, Eleanor."

"Oh, well, that makes it better. You just left me?" She stepped back, but he quickly closed the distance between them.

"It wasn't real. The phony gun is the cigarette lighter from Clines's desk. I recognized it right away." He spread his arms, and she stepped into them as if drawn by a magnet. "You weren't in any danger. Like I said, King's a dolt. A thief, a jerk, and a dolt."

"Oh." Her heart pattered. Her arms hung limp at her sides. What should she do with her arms? She'd only imagined being held by this man, and in her wildest dreams she always knew what to do with every part of her body. "But, if the gun was a fake, why didn't you…" She glanced away. He could've immediately rescued her.

He lifted her chin. "I'm sorry if you were frightened. I'd heard enough of your sparring with King to know you were holding your own."

"I was more concerned about getting locked in this vault."

His caress along her chin ramped up the beats per minute of her heart.

"Is it so bad?" His hand returned to her waist.

She smiled, staring into his teasing gray eyes. Bringing her arms up, she tentatively encircled his shoulders.

"I went back up to alert Cline so he could get the cops

rolling and intercept King before he made his getaway. He's probably being handcuffed right now."

"And you came back down…" She held her breath with her thought. He didn't have to come back, to get locked in the vault with her.

"Our rescue is coming shortly. There isn't much time."

"Time?" She could stand here touching him for all the time they had. But—

"I went back up for another reason besides speaking to Cline. There was something I needed to get." One hand fell from her and slipped into his jacket pocket. He smiled, winked, and lifted a sprig of mistletoe over their heads. "I couldn't let King's kiss be the last you remember from tonight." He held her closer. "I've wanted to do this for ages." His lips touched hers and then retreated, asking her permission.

Reaching, walking her fingertips up the back of his neck, she laced them together. His breath was moist, tinged with the scent of chocolate and brandy. "Just what *are* your intentions?"

"May I kiss you, Eleanor?"

"Oh, yes"—she tilted her lips toward his—"Roman, Jack Roman."

A Tropical Holiday

She had one wish for Christmas. Peace. Not the world kind of peace. Inner peace. Yuma Camry needed to forget the divorce from a lifeless marriage and find herself once again. She snorted. Wow, did that sound corny. But it was the truth, damn it.

After giving up lying on the beach under a gray sky at her hotel, she'd opted for a guided tour. Now, sitting at the back of the bus, she rested her forehead against the window, breathing the cool outside air seeping in around the window seal and trying to avoid the combined breath wafting from the gabby couple in the seat in front of her. They'd obviously enjoyed the local specialty—salsa rich with cilantro and onions. A fish in an oxygen-deprived aquarium would have more fresh air. She sighed and glanced outside at thick green foliage of trees, bushes, and vines whizzing by.

Her sister, Setty, hadn't exactly cheered her on when she'd announced her Christmas vacation plans. Well-meaning, still-married Setty told her that a trip to Cancun, Mexico, solo, might be rash, yet she hadn't tried to talk her out of her one-person holiday. In fact, Yuma thought her sister envied her a bit, taking off by herself. How romantic. There's romantic and there's romance. Yuma had insisted reflection was her goal, not romance. Setty had given her that oh-sure-whatever-you-say smile. It did no good to argue with her sister who believed all the important things in life like sex, kids, mowed lawns, and a well-tuned auto required a man. She didn't need what Setty needed.

But...if a little romance came her way, a slight distraction from reflection, then that would be fine.

The bus slowed along the main street of a small town. Franco, the tour guide, gave a running commentary on village life in Mexico. His reindeer headband bobbed when he laughed at his own jokes. They picked up speed, and a few moments later approached the entrance to the ruins of Tulum, one of the last cities inhabited by Maya people, and spread along cliffs overlooking the ocean.

Yuma looked at the backs of her fellow tourists' heads. And they came in twos: old couples, young couples, a male couple, and two elderly English ladies who kept asking the guide personal questions and turning around to smile at Yuma every few miles. The empty seat beside her became a neon sign announcing *this woman in her forties is alone*. Well, she was just very twenty-first century, traveling without a companion.

Although, it would've been okay to see someone else sightseeing alone, someone who would perhaps have found her interesting enough to chance a...friendship.

But no single, middle-aged, American professor existed who specialized in Mayan history and would ask her to his room after the tour to share a bottle of wine, who would find her irresistible long into the night and serve her breakfast at dawn.

"You will enjoy the tour, even if Mexico is unreasonably cold." Franco laughed heartily at his play on words as the bus pulled into the parking lot. Day two in sunny Mexico remained chilly and cloudy, exactly like day one. Guaranteed warmth should've accompanied the high price of a winter holiday vacation. The door to the bus swooshed open with a screech, welcoming in damp ocean air. This Christmas was salty scents instead of pine…

Hugging her jean jacket to her, Yuma stepped off the bus and into the arms of the two English ladies, one on each side, looping their arms around hers.

"Hello, dearie. We saw you were alone and thought you should chum with us. I'm Maureen." Her white hair glowed like a halo around her head as she gazed over rectangular gold-framed glasses perched on a nose not quite in the middle of her face. Bright hazel eyes smiled under fluttering white lashes. The warmth of her bony fingers penetrated the jean jacket covering Yuma's arm. "This is my baby sister, Helen."

Helen tugged slightly on her, forcing Yuma to shift her attention to the plumper face of the baby sister. Faded blue eyes stared up while a whiskered upper lip curled in a smile, reminding Yuma of a baby seal in a Disney movie she took her niece to see. Helen patted her arm. "We single birds have to stick together."

Although she'd have preferred to continue the tour alone with only her thoughts, Yuma couldn't manage to disengage from the sisters. Resigned, she joined the single birds and followed Franco around the grounds of Tulum, learning bits of Mayan history sprinkled with tour guide humor, the best of which amused Yuma and eluded the English sisterhood. They stayed at the front of the group for Helen's sake, partly deaf in her left ear, according to Maureen, thanks to a bloody kick to the head from a mongrel cousin when she was four.

In spite of a gray sky, the Mayan ruins were beautiful, set on cliffs dotted with green and overlooking a foamy shoreline. But she had little time to think. When Franco wasn't expounding, the sister birds were chirping in her ear.

"Have you been single long?" baby sister Helen asked

when the tour concluded for lunch. "You leave him, or did he leave you for a younger woman?"

"Helen! Don't be so nosey."

Helen's seal lips pouted, and her round eyes grew watery. "I only meant to make conversation, Miss Bossy. You came up with the younger woman scenario anyway." She took a huge triumphant bite out of her cheese sandwich.

"Well!" Maureen turned to Yuma. "Sorry, dearie, but…"

"No need." Yuma waved off the explanation. "I think I wear divorced like a badge. Or maybe a scary mask."

"Oh, nonsense," Maureen said. "A sweet, young thing like you? There must be all sorts of opportunity for romance."

Yuma smiled at the sweet, young thing description. "I don't really care about romance."

"Romance is highly overrated." Helen nodded, mouth full of sandwich, hurt feelings apparently forgotten. "In this day and age, you can get more than romance if you aren't careful."

Maureen clucked her tongue and gave her sister a scornful look.

Yuma knew a middle-aged redhead in the commercial loan department at work who would agree with Helen. She would've preferred to bring back a case of pineapples from Hawaii rather than her case of herpes. But Helen needn't worry. This Mexican vacation, solo style, was not a desperation samba. Yuma needed some time alone—that was all.

Still… If yesterday, walking the streets of old Cancun, shopping the Mercado, and eating lunch on the patio of a restaurant under cloudy skies, she'd met someone, it would've been okay. But no young Don Juan had plied her with tequila and seduced her into getting a tattoo on her hip while caressing her cheek and murmuring what a fascinating creature she was.

"No more romance for you, Helen?" Yuma crumpled her napkin and stuffed it into her empty paper cup. The notion of romance finding Helen seemed more remote than the idea Helen could even know what dangers lurked in a careless flirtatious union.

"Oh, if it were true romance, I wouldn't walk away from it." She scrubbed mayonnaise from her whiskers. "I've had my share though, dearie. It's Maureen here that's always on the lookout for a man. The marrying kind."

"Helen, really!" The older sister stood and carried her lunch container to the trashcan.

More composed when she returned to the table, she didn't sit down again. "You'll have to excuse my sister. She has no sense of propriety." She peered over her glasses and gave her sister an obviously long-practiced scowl, a speechless language understood between siblings.

"I think they're loading the bus." Yuma stood and tossed her lunch remnants into the trashcan. "Thanks for the company. Have a Merry Christmas." Walking away from the sisters, she was glad Franco had instructed everyone to return to their same seats. Chumming with Helen could be amusing, but Maureen—not so much.

Yuma was the fifth one back in her seat. The two men quietly bickered, sitting as far apart as the bus seating would allow, one of them hanging a butt cheek off the edge of the aisle seat. Gabby couple clumped together, silently. Mr. had his head back and his eyes closed, rubbing his bulbous abdomen. When she sat, she considered if she needed someone in her life. Walking away from a twenty-year marriage proved she didn't. She certainly could do without the arguing or the nursemaid duties men seemed to require. No, that was unfair. She'd had one marriage, one man. Maybe they didn't all demand nursemaids. Mrs. Gabby

Couple opened a package of antacid tablets, took out two, and placed them on Mr.'s extended tongue.

It's always easier to figure out what you don't need. The trick is figuring out what you do need.

Maybe all husbands weren't selfish, unimaginative, reticent, and clueless. She was hard pressed to think of any of the men she knew who weren't. Leaning her head back, she stared at the ceiling. Maybe Dr. Tanner, her optometrist. Or Carl in accounting. Not knowing either one on a personal level, she could imagine them to be different from the husbands she actually knew. Could Dr. Tanner look into his wife's eyes without checking for glaucoma? Could he see the soul without seeing the iris?

What exactly had she expected to gain from this trip? Turning her head, she looked out at gray skies and sighed. She'd expected to get some damn sun in Mexico and lie on the beach in the bright yellow two-piece swimsuit that cost too much. Time to adjust and be alone. Then again, if some younger-than-she-was hunk happened to notice her and find her attractive, she'd be like Helen and not walk, or swim, away. She closed her eyes and rested her head against the window. A little sun, a little adventure, a little…

"Do you mind?" A deep voice asked as he settled into the seat beside her. A mellow, woodsy scent rose from his skin.

"Oh…no, go ahead." Yuma turned her face toward the friendly drawl in time to see the back of his head as he bent over to stow a backpack under the seat. The empty seat beside her suddenly overflowed with warmth. His amber colored hair covered his neck and brushed at the shoulders straining against a waffle-weave shirt.

"Man, am I glad there's an empty seat." Straightening, he smiled, raking his hand through his hair. Yuma wished her hair would fall in such full waves around her face. "I missed my tour bus back to hotel row." He scratched the beginnings of a beard, then stroked downward as if to smooth it into place. "Hi. I'm Eirik." He offered his hand.

Eirik's firm handshake heated her core, his skin just rough enough to prove he had no fear of manual labor. "Yuma."

"Great name. Very visual." His smile brightened the gray day. "And I'll bet there's a story behind it."

"Of sorts."

"Come on." He turned slightly toward her and pushed broad shoulders against the bus seat as if getting comfy in an overstuffed chair. "Tell me a story."

His persona was an open invitation she couldn't ignore. "I was conceived in a rest stop outside Yuma, Arizona," she blurted without a second thought. "In my parents' younger days, they traveled around in a VW bus."

"Wow." He thumped his chest with his fist. "That's a great story. It has lust, adventure, romance, and love all compacted into two sentences."

What was the little flutter in her chest? His description sounded exactly the way she'd always felt about her beginnings into this world. She stared into eyes the same amber color as his hair. Although he had to be at least ten years her junior, his eyes were ageless, old and knowing, youthful and laughing. Her heart overrode her head with the notion she'd known these eyes forever.

"What about Eirik? Is there a story behind your name?"

"It's a Norse name." He laughed. "That creates a picture, doesn't it? But the only story is the one I'm creating." He glanced out the window. The bus pulled away from the parking lot. "Tulum was great. So many revenants standing guard on their history, overlooking the sea."

"You believe in ghosts?"

His gaze swept her face. He traced her lips, stared into

each of her eyes. A slow smile blanketed his face. "You do, too."

Maybe she did. She'd never considered the subject beyond the Hollywood movie, rattling chain kind. Why hadn't she looked among the broken stones to see the ghosts of Tulum?

"Tulum." He rested his head against the top of the seat and stared into the air above them. "A visual. Large transparent circle with a solid tower rising out of it in a swoop, spreading at the top and disappearing from sight." Mesmerized, Yuma watched him draw the vision with his hands. She smelled the dust of the ruins and his earthy scent. Gazing into the air he drew his vision from, she wondered what he'd been smoking.

"Words are great, aren't they? Some words evoke great shapes. Like Tulum."

"Shapes?"

"Yeah, some words take shape. For instance, mellow looks like a double camel's hump. Cracker is a little jagged point and then two larger jagged points and then a splintered line. Laughter is a round exploding circle with a dangling tail."

Yuma laughed. "I'm sorry." She laughed more. "You're a little crazy."

He laughed with her. "Yeah, but you're the only one who knows." He touched her arm. "Really, you're the only person I've ever told. Some words have shape. I *see* them."

His hand slid down her arm and back to his lap. Feathery ripples followed in the wake of his fingertips. Yuma thought his hand could've stayed on her arm longer.

He leaned closer. "And some words have stories. Entire stories in one word. Like Yuma."

"Complete stories?" She breathed deeply, inhaling him. Her peripheral vision closed to a pinpoint filled with Eirik's face and the amber color of his hair.

"Not always. Stories in the works. Stories unfolding."

"Is the story of Yuma still unfolding?" Her whispered words swirled the air between them.

"I think there are whole blank pages to fill." He tilted his chin and cocked a brow. "How inventive did your parents get with your siblings' names?"

"I have one sister we call Setty, short for Settled."

"Oh, poor Setty." He chuckled.

"Yes, well, she is their testament to giving up the bus and finding roots."

"And does Setty live up to her name?"

"Rooted." Her sister had always been the straight and narrow, stay at home kind. "Do you think it was pre-destination?"

"How can we say?"

Eirik reached under his seat and pulled a bottle of water from his pack. "Drink?"

"No thanks."

His lips were wet and glistening as he replaced the cap. A small water drop hung from the corner of his mouth, and she imagined wiping the droplet with her finger, feeling the wet softness. He brushed his fingertips across his lips and winked at her before turning his attention to the tops of the ruins peeking above the trees. Had he read her mind? Her face flushed warm as the two English sisters peered at her from the front of the bus. She couldn't hear what Franco said. The blood rushing to her head was too noisy. Or was that the engine of the bus coming to life?

The bus bumped onto the main road.

"That was great!" Eirik said.

They turned toward the window to get one last look at the ruins before a thick leafy barricade blocked the vision.

He smiled, nodding his head as if bidding farewell to

unseen friends. "Silent to all but those who hear." Reaching under his seat, he replaced the water bottle in his backpack.

"And what do you hear?" She hadn't listened and wished she had.

"I could say the lives of those before me, but I think it's more my own inner voice ricocheting off the generations." He shook his head, and she wanted to touch his hair. "Yuma, you make me say things I say to no one else. Are you a witch?"

"I could be a witch." Witch and bewitching. *This young man with exotic ideas thinks I'm a witch.* Could she weave a lusty spell? What shape would he give to lust?

"I think you are. You know me, and we've only just met. It's difficult to get past the lust and see it, but I'm sure we know each other quite well."

The witch was an amber-haired man who read minds. "Lust?"

"Lust for life. People who travel alone, especially during the holidays, are adventure seekers, overcome with too much lust to share their road with less romantic souls."

What if a like romantic soul came along? Could you know someone in a half dozen sentences, who opened doors you'd not broached in years, then put to words your vague ideas? Yuma stared into his serious ageless eyes. Romance and romantic. Love and lust. Words with shapes. Now that she understood there were blank pages of her life, they would be easy to write. Easier than erasing—which was what she had been attempting to do. Lust for life.

"Where are you, Yuma?"

"I'm...thinking." She'd lost her lust somewhere. "The shape of—"

"Lust?" He leaned his head back and closed his eyes. "An opaque bubble, opaque because it's filled with white smoke." He opened one eye like a very young, cute Popeye and smiled. "Go ahead. Try to see it."

Yuma leaned her head back and closed her eyes. A gigantic bubble floated overhead, the white smoke swirling inside. It fit. She stepped gently into the smoke. When the bus slowed and came to a stop, her eyes remained shut, and her hearing deaf to Franco's words. She felt Eirik stir beside her, then his mouth against her ear.

"Goodbye, Yuma."

She jerked upright. "Why?"

"More to explore." He stood and nodded toward the window.

She looked out to a bus stop along the dirt road of a Mexican village. As she opened her mouth to question, he appeared outside below the window. The bus groaned as the driver shifted to pull away from the stop.

Eirik made writing motions in the air, and she read his lips, "keep writing." Blowing her a kiss and waving, he disappeared in a faint cloud of dust as the bus pulled away.

The vehicle hit a larger than ever rut in the road. Yuma's head bounced twice off the window.

"Damn!" She laughed out loud and looked around. Franco's antlers sat crookedly on his head. Half of the gay couple had fallen from his perch on the edge of the seat. The English single birds were clutching each other. Yuma turned back to the scene out her window, but it had changed. She craned her neck to spy behind the bus. But the village had been eaten up by the cloud of dust.

She sighed, a bit disoriented, gazing out the window as the bus picked up speed on the blacktop, returning her to the resort. A flash of light danced across the chrome on the back of the seat in front of her—the clouds parted for the first time since she'd landed in Mexico.

****

The sunlight soaked her with warmth when she descended the steps to the white, silky sands of the beach. She wore the yellow swimsuit she'd paid too much for but clutched the oversized towel around her against the chill of the ocean breeze. Sunbathers were sparse, and a choice of lounge chairs stood available. Dragging one to face the aqua waves, she sat on the edge, huddled under the towel, and listened for revenants floating on the ocean breezes. If Eirik were beside her…her lids drooped shut, and she pictured the word *ocean*.

"You won't get much sun like that, but you're probably warmer than I am."

She opened her eyes to the voice. A man about her age straightened a lounger next to hers and reclined. His jet-black hair, cropped short, reflected sunlight as if sparks danced across his head. Smile lines bracketed his mouth.

"The sun is luscious, but the air is still a bit chilly for me." She shivered as a draft of salty air tickled her exposed calves.

In spite of his relaxed position, goosebumps prickled his muscled arms. "Yeah, I kind of had a toasty, beach vacation in mind myself. Then again, this beats the snow I left behind in Minneapolis. White sand trumps white snow for me this Christmas." He laughed. "You took the Tulum tour this morning, didn't you?"

"I did. How did you know?"

"I saw you get off the bus." His hands fidgeted on the arms of the lounger. "Are you alone?"

"Yep, that's me. Alone." And she didn't mind at all.

"So am I." His blue eyes sparkled like the sun on the ocean. "We're fellow adventure seekers."

Her heart thumped. "Funny you say that." She swung her legs around to the side to face him.

"Why?"

"Someone called me that earlier today." Under the towel she pinched herself. *Ouch*. "I'm of the mind that adventure seekers have a strong lust for life."

"And funny you should say that."

"Why?"

"Someone used those same words to me last night at happy hour." He heaved his bronze shoulders off the lounger and sat on the edge, his knees coming into contact with hers. "Do you believe in coincidence?"

"No." She stared into his face. Moments passed. A seagull sang overhead. A woman called to her daughter who'd gone too close to the water.

"Would you like to take a walk, see what the breeze blows our way?"

"Yes." She stood, unfurled one of her arms and smiled. "I think it's actually warming up."

His glance registered the yellow swimsuit, and she was happy she'd paid too much. He rose and stepped closer. A seagull squawked above. "My name's Fisher."

"Unusual. I wonder if there's a story attached."

"How did you know?" The seagull repeated his call overhead.

She chuckled. "Oh, lucky guess." She glanced at the gull, floating on the air current overhead. Or riding on the shoulders of a revenant? "My name is Yuma."

"As unusual a name as mine. I bet your name has a story behind it too."

"Of sorts." They strolled away from the loungers. "But if I tell you, you'll have to help me fill some blank pages of my story."

"I can do that."

No Room at the Inn

Sadi Anne peered through the snow-spattered windshield at the neon sign. Between swipes of the wiper blades, she read the yellow lights—Bethle Heights Motel. Sort of. The sputtering neon on several of the letters gave the only hotel in the town of the same name new meaning—Bethle He M.

"I sure as hell hope there's room at the inn. This would be worth a laugh if I wasn't in such a foul mood. Bah humbug." She spoke into the air. Why couldn't Christmas be postponed once in a while? It came every year whether she liked it or not.

Aiming for what she hoped was the snow-covered driveway into the parking lot of the motel, she took her foot off the gas, turned the steering wheel slightly, and slid more than coasted to a stop. Cars, lined up in parking spots two deep, were a good ten yards ahead. Where to park? She'd be in the elements no matter where she chose. "Not even a covered check-in area. Merry ho-ho Christmas, Sadi Anne."

At the edge of the building, a spotlight on the roof lit an area next to the dumpster. *A light from above shows the way.* She snickered. *I'm so profound.* The area appeared to be the best chance of getting out of the path of any other cars that might slide into the lot. "At least I'm not on a camel." She eased her beloved, old Z4 alongside the trash bin, shifted into park, and turned off the wipers. "Sorry, baby." She patted the dashboard and stared at the snow accumulating on the windshield, reluctant to leave the warmth of the car. Then she squared her shoulders and pushed out a breath. "Well, heck, it isn't going to get any better out there."

After popping the trunk, she pulled her jacket and neck scarf from the back seat, shrugged into protection from the elements, and opened the car door. She set her booted feet on the ground. As fast as she could move through the ankle-deep snow, she skirted around to the trunk. Leaving the larger case and camera bag behind, she trudged to the front door with her overnight case slung over her shoulder, muttering to herself. "Yeah, Sadi, this is what you get for volunteering to work the weekend before Christmas. You get to play photographer right along with your reporting. Anything to avoid all the holiday parties. Yeah, great idea."

Inside the surprisingly roomy lobby, she stamped her feet on a green doormat emblazoned with the faces of nine reindeer, bells hanging from their antlers, and one of them sporting a red nose. After ruffling her short curls to remove the cold flakes, she dusted snow from her coat shoulders and loosened the scarf from around her neck. A fragrant fire burned in a stone fireplace in one corner. Several people sat in worn, plush chairs at odd angles to the warmth drinking from cups, chatting, or reading. A table along a wall held coffee pots, hot water dispenser, and packages of tea and chocolate along with plates of cookies. Next to that was a Christmas tree—a *real* Christmas tree—decorated in red and green.

Inhaling the scents, she turned toward the registration desk. She couldn't escape the holiday fanfare, but at least no one knew her and wouldn't implore her to be jolly and festive.

"Good evening." A round faced, olive-skinned man with

an accent greeted her. "Merry Christmas."

She ignored the cheeriness. "Sadi Fleming. I have a reservation for three nights."

"Oh?" His smooth skin wrinkled across his forehead. He tapped his computer keyboard.

She tapped her toe

"I think all of our guests have checked in." Red and green lights strung overhead glittered his slick, black hair as he shook his head.

"But I haven't. What are you saying?"

"I am not seeing your name, Ms. Fleming. Were you staying with someone, perhaps under a different name?"

"No. Just me. Sadi Anne Fleming." Alarm bells, not jingle bells, sounded in her head. "Well, I'm here now. Can I please have a room?"

"I wish I could accommodate you, but we are full. There's a tournament tomorrow—"

"I know. That's why I'm here."

Large, brown, sympathetic eyes blinked but nothing issued from his mouth.

"You're the only motel here, right?"

"Yes. I am so sorry." His sing-song accent dripped with empathy.

"But I called. I made a reservation."

"Did you receive an email confirmation?"

"You do confirmations? It's not like you're a big hotel chain. I didn't receive one and didn't expect one. The woman who took my reservation didn't ask me for my email address. But I spoke to a *real* person who made me a *real* reservation for a *real room*." She realized her pitch had reached panic level, but this man had to understand her predicament…and fix it.

"Again, I apologize."

Her overnight case pulled heavy on her shoulder, and

she let it fall to the floor. The room had gone hot and stuffy. She unzipped her coat. "What am I going to do? I can't go back out in that weather." She shook her arm, half numb from toting the case, toward the window.

"I could call a hotel in Payson. Maybe the snow will let up—"

"Not until sometime after midnight." She thumped the counter. "I've checked. And Payson is an hour away. I'm supposed to cover the tournament. I—"

"Excuse me." A quiet voice accompanied a nudge to her arm. "You can stay with me."

Sadi jerked around. "Wh-what?"

A young woman with smiling, sky-blue eyes and a heavily freckled nose met her gaze. "I couldn't help but overhear your problem."

She glanced beyond the young woman and was met with numerous pairs of eyes. Apparently, the entire lobby gave witness to her desperation. The people sitting around the fireplace had paused their reading and conversations to watch Sadi and the hotel clerk. Her face heated at the realization she'd inadvertently become the center of attention. "Was I shouting?"

Her would-be rescuer patted her arm. "Not really. Don't worry about it. But I can help. I'm in the tournament tomorrow, and it's exciting to have a real news person here for us. My brother and I have a suite. Two bedrooms. You can stay with me in the half with two beds."

"Oh my gosh. That's…that's so nice of you. But, I, uh, you don't even know me."

"And you don't know us, but don't worry. My brother is really nice. He'll be fine with it. And we're like normal people and all." She glanced back at the audience.

"Don't go out in the weather again." A woman waved her hand. "Stay, dear."

"They're very nice people." A bearded man bobbed his head.

A guy in a ballcap and plaid shirt raised his cocoa cup as if toasting. "They're cool, man."

Apparently, the audience was trying to help.

She timidly smiled and ducked her head. "Well, okay, then. My name is Sadi Fleming."

"I'm Mary Jones." They shook hands. Mary's auburn hair was pulled back in a ponytail. Her full bangs bobbed when her head matched the motion of her handshaking.

"You're a life saver, Mary. But shouldn't we ask your brother first?"

"Believe me. It's okay. He's not here right now." She picked up Sadi's overnight case without effort. They were both about the same height at five-feet-five, but Mary had a little more bulk to her which translated to strength. She appeared to be about twenty years old. "Is this all the luggage you have?"

"No, there's a larger bag and a camera case in my trunk."

"Bubba can get them when he gets back." She turned to the hotel clerk. "Can we get another key card for room 144?"

"Of course, ma'am."

With key card in hand, she followed her newfound friend, glancing at the audience as they passed. Several individuals gave her a thumbs-up. Others smiled, nodded, and turned back to their activities. She waved and caught up with Mary.

"I can't tell you how much I appreciate this."

"You're welcome. I'm pretty jazzed to have the press stay with me." Her freckles glittered her face when she smiled. "You're a photographer *and* journalist?"

"Not normally. But since it's the weekend before Christmas I volunteered to be both." Dragging a photographer along who could've either been too cheery with the season, or too morose missing festivities at home would've only made her weekend more miserable.

"Maybe Bubba can help you. He's a freelance photographer."

"Oh?" Her heart constricted. Alex was a freelance photographer. *After three years you'd think I'd be over him.*

"What newspaper are you with?"

She followed her around a corner and down another hallway. "The Arizona Republic."

"Wow, that's the biggest. So, you're a sports reporter?"

"No. I do interest stories. I cover anything unique, such as the *first* women's curling competition in Arizona."

Mary beamed. "I'm so excited. This could lead to the Olympics. Who knows?"

Sadi's heart thumped, catching her enthusiasm. "Are you one of the star players?"

"It's really a team effort." She stopped at room 144 and inserted the key card. "But let's just say, I'm good." With a shove at the door, she sighed. "And I'd have never guessed this could happen. It's like a dream come true. Come on in."

They entered a small sitting area furnished with a couch and chair. On the other side of a breakfast bar, a sink, microwave, and refrigerator formed a kitchen. After shrugging out of her coat and hanging it on a coat tree next to the door, she followed Mary past a bathroom on the left, and an opened door straight ahead. The full-sized bed indicated the room for big brother. They hung a right into another bedroom.

"I've already piled my stuff on this bed, if that's okay."

"Hey, beggars can't be choosers." She plopped onto the bed closest to the window. "I'll reimburse you for the room."

Mary set her case on the floor. "No need. I'm happy to have you here. Would you like a soda and some chips? I'm a snacker."

Her stomach rumbled at the mention of food. She hadn't eaten anything since lunch, and then only a small burger on the run. "Yes, please."

Back in the front room, Sadi tucked into a corner of the couch.

The young woman lifted two cans from the fridge and two snack-sized bags of potato chips from a cupboard. "Hope these are okay. Bubba and I like the same things, so we didn't get a variety." She relaxed on the other end of the couch.

"Anything is fine." Sadi popped the tab. "So, tell me about your dream come true."

"I'd have to start with Christmas three years ago when I was a senior in high school. I was in a horrible auto accident." Mary tore open her chip bag. "They had to remove my spleen and my thyroid was damaged." She crunched on a chip with the nonchalance of someone on the other side of a tragedy handled.

"Oh, no. How awful. Here in Bethle Heights?"

"No, Payson, where we lived."

Sadi sipped the fizzy cola, her mind wandering to Alex again. He'd been from Payson.

"I ended up in Sacramento for treatment and rehab. My brother did the research and insisted it was the best place to be. He moved with me."

"Wow. He sounds like a great brother."

"He is. But the timing was right. If the timing can be right for a life changing accident. Bubba had had his heart broken. I really worried about him. Moving with me, having to be so involved with my medical issues, totally consumed him and helped him step away from his heartache. I don't think he ever really got over her. I wish I'd known her. I would've punched her in the nose. We were supposed to meet her that Christmas, but she dumped him."

Sadi's cola pooled in her mouth, bubbles popping on her tongue with each snapshot memory. She and Alex broke up at Christmas right before she was supposed to meet his family. She stared, not seeing the freckled face until Mary's cheery voice continued.

"Long story short, one of my therapists was a curler, and she got me hooked on it. When we moved back to Payson, I found out there was a small curling club." She munched a chip.

"It's not so small now." Sadi forced the words, trying to bury the recollections. "Did you have something to do with that?"

Mary beamed. "I think so."

"And where is your brother? Surely not out in this snowstorm."

"Yeah, afraid so. I'm such a ditz sometimes. I forgot my meds. I can't skip them because of my missing spleen and thyroid issues. But there's a drugstore in town that could get me enough for a couple of days, so we didn't have to go all the way into Payson."

Sadi glanced toward the window overlooking a courtyard. Snow still drifted down. "I guess this is the perfect weather for curling…and Christmas." As if the cold reality of the holiday sapped all her energy, the corners of her mouth tugged downward.

"Oh dear. Something tells me you don't want to be covering this event. Are you missing some holiday events? Maybe with family?"

"Nooo." Poor young lady looked like she could shed tears being the cause of her distress. "I'm more than happy to be here. It's…it's this time of year. The holidays, Christmas." She waved a hand through the air, hoping to wave away the direction of the conversation.

"You don't like Christmas?" Her chin dropped, mouth open. Her incredulity bordered on comic.

"I lost someone I loved shortly before Christmas a few years back. This whole cheery season is sour for me now."

"Oh no, I'm so sorry. Did someone die, your husband, or maybe your mom?"

Sadi choked on a swallow of cola. Shaking her head, she wiped the corner of her mouth. "No one died. Sorry I said it that way. My boyfriend dumped me. I thought maybe he'd be my husband someday, but he found someone else when I followed a job to New York."

"Oh-oh." Mary scooted closer and patted her shoulder.

"And fast too. That's what hurt so much." Why she was compelled to tell her sad story to a stranger puzzled her. But she sensed a sweet understanding in Mary and closeness, as if she should've been in her life all along.

"You aren't wearing a wedding ring. You haven't found anyone else?"

Sadi abandoned her chips and set the bag on the end table. Dragging up the hurt robbed her of any desire for munchies. "No. I haven't had time. Too busy working and…" Why make excuses for a heart not yet healed.

"Isn't this strange? You and my brother had the same experience." Her brows rose. She rubbed her knuckles against her lips. "Bubba is still single too." She tipped her head, a mischievous glint in her eye. "This is the reason you didn't have a room." She scooted to the edge of the couch. "You and Bubba are meant to meet!"

The last thing she needed was a forced hook up with a lonely heart at Christmas. "I doubt your brother—"

A loud crash came from outside.

In unison, they jumped off the couch and ran to the window in her brother's bedroom that looked out on the parking lot. At the corner of the building, a huge red truck had crushed her precious Z4 into the garbage dumpster.

"No, no, no! Not my car." Sadi threw her hands to her face, her fingers threaded into the curls framing her face.

"Oh! Oh! That looks like…oh no…that's Bubba." Mary dashed to the door before she'd finished speaking.

Sadi snatched her coat and another she assumed was Mary's and trotted behind her. Fleeing the room, they charged down the hall and into the lobby. She flung the young curler's coat at her as she pushed through the people milling around the front door inside. Sadi followed in her wake as if plunging through a wave that closed in behind them. Mary charged outside. Sadi's feet slid twice, and she nearly went down, but Mary grabbed her arm.

As they reached the truck, three men gathered at the driver's side and opened the door. Sadi felt an inappropriate laugh gurgle in her throat. The men wore matching royal blue sweatshirts with "Wise Men Electric" embroidered across the shoulders. A bowling ball crashed through pins below the team name.

"Bubba, Bubba, are you okay?" Her new friend tried to see over the three wise men.

"No blood," one of the men reported. "But he's unconscious. Must've hit his head on the door window with the jolt when the air bag deployed. Inside the truck shows no damage or blood. Let's get him out of the cold and into the motel."

Moving him might not be smart. "Wait." Sadi tapped on one of the men's shoulders. "Shouldn't we call for paramedics?"

"We *are* paramedics. Off duty, but we can handle this. Give us room."

She gripped Mary's arm and pulled her back while the three men maneuvered Bubba out of the truck. Keeping him as level as possible, one held his head and shoulders, one in the middle, and one took his feet. As they passed by, the overhead spotlight lit the face of the unconscious man.

Sadi gasped. "Alex?" Stunned, her feet didn't move when the procession headed for the lobby.

At the door, her new friend waved a hurry up signal. "Sadi, come on."

With effort she trudged back through the snow. Confusion muddled her thoughts like she'd come into the middle of a complicated movie plot she couldn't sort out. Inside, they'd laid him on a couch in the lobby. She joined Mary at one end of the sofa. The worried sister gripped her hand.

He looked the same as three years ago. Blond hair was tousled and in need of a cut as it always was. His shoulders were just as broad, his waist narrow, and his hands—oh his hands—large and strong, rested by his sides.

One of the men took his pulse and checked under his eyelids. "He's fine. Might have a mild concussion but—"

At that moment, he stirred. A moan came from the lips she could never forget. His brow furrowed, and his lids slowly revealed the deep blue of a stormy, summer sky.

"Bubba?" Mary lurched forward and gripped his hand.

His eyes opened, gazing over her head and directly into Sadi's face. He blinked. "Am I dead?"

"Bubba!"

"Oh. I must not be." He shifted his focus to his sister. "Carina Ballerina. I think I might've crashed a car. And it looked like—"

"Yeah, my car, Alex!"

He blinked again; his brows nearly touched in the center with a frown of confusion. "Where did you come from, Sadi Anne?"

"The better question is where have *you* been, Alex?"

Carina or Mary, or whoever she was, jerked her head

back and forth looking between them, her eyes blinking like fluttering Christmas tree lights. "You two know each other?"

Sadi's heart tripped. As if reindeer trampled all the moisture from her mouth, she could manage only a raspy, "Yes."

Several guests returned to seats around the fireplace, but no conversation resumed, their attention locked on the scene in the middle of the lobby.

"This is surreal." He pushed onto his elbows to sit.

"No, no, Bubba." Mary patted his shoulder.

"I'm fine, Carina. Right, guys?" He swung his legs over the edge of the sofa.

"Do you feel dizzy or nauseous?"

"Nope. Just foolish."

One of the wise men pointed a finger at him. "I'm in room 308 if you start feeling at all sick. No matter the time, call if you do. But I think you'll be fine."

"Thanks." A meek handwave followed his appreciation as the three men retreated to the table laden with coffee and cookies. "So…"

Sadi tapped her foot, fingers digging into her hips where her hands gripped. "So?"

Alex rose slowly, pivoting to face her fully. Mary clung to his arm as if he might topple over any moment.

"Seeing you here…" He rubbed a hand across his forehead as if checking his temperature. "I thought that crash sent me into the twilight zone."

"You've got some explaining to do."

"Me?" He splayed a hand across his chest. "Me?" The veins at his temple pulsed with the familiar rhythm of annoyance she remembered. "You left me."

"I-I…it wasn't like that." Her eyes burned. She would not cry. After three years, no way.

Alex heaved a breath. He wavered, or was her vision

watery with threatening tears?

"Bubba, sit down a minute." Mary tugged him back to the couch, then with pleading eyes wiggled a come-here finger at Sadi. "You sit too." She touched her brother's cheek in such a loving gesture, Sadi nearly lost her battle with crying.

Instead, she sucked air and sat as far from lost love as she could. As much as her legs said run, her heart defied the urge. If nothing else, she wanted to know why he'd gotten over her so fast that he hightailed it to California not long after she'd moved. Where to begin? *Find your voice, Sadi. You always said you'd let him have it if you ever saw him again.*

She dared a glance past Mary who sat between them. Alex's jaw clenched and unclenched. He ran a hand through his hair.

"Well?" Sadi said.

He slapped a hand on his thigh. "You first."

"Me first what?" She wouldn't make it easy for him. Not after breaking her heart in a million pieces.

"Oh, come on."

"Really?"

He shot up. "This isn't going to work."

She jumped up and thrust a finger over Mary's head and in his direction. "You couldn't find a way to make it work then either."

A gasp came from somewhere near the fireplace.

Mary snatched her fingers out of the air with one hand and grabbed her brother's arm with the other. "Just stop." The mild-mannered young lady's voice snapped, taking Sadi by surprise. "You're both being stubborn. Sit down! Now!" She tugged them back to the couch.

Sadi's breath came in short puffs as if she'd run laps around the lobby. She sneaked a peek at Alex. His jaw worked like he was sucking on a piece of Christmas candy.

Whispers drifted from the people around the fireplace. She glanced toward the exit. Should she escape? The snow fall had thickened. Her car might not even start. Trapped. Trapped with a man who'd dumped her at Christmas. How would she ever get through *this* Christmas?

"Okay, then. I'll start." Mary's sweet tone returned but with a firm conviction. "You obviously know each other. I think something happened three years ago, and I want to know what."

She couldn't do this. Scooting forward, she braced to stand, but Mary still clung to her hand. "No, you don't, Sadi."

The corner of Alex's mouth tipped up.

"Don't look so smug, Bubba. You start."

"Carina—"

"Don't Carina Ballerina me. What happened and when?"

He glared at Mary, a growl deep in his throat. "Three years ago, this is the woman I planned to propose to on Christmas Day. But she chose a job offer over me, and I never heard from her again."

Mary turned a scowl on her.

"That's—" Her throat constricted.

"Well?" The protective sister wouldn't let her off the hook.

"You could've *told* me you were going to propose."

"Would it have made a difference?"

How could she answer that? She would've begged him harder to join her. That's not what he wanted to hear. But she never planned to be separated from him forever.

"Yeah, I thought so." He ran a hand down his face as if the subject tired him. "You obviously didn't feel like I did."

"How can you say that? I wanted you to come with me. I begged you to."

"New York?" He shook his head, his mouth squinched

like the word was nasty tasting.

"You can work anywhere freelancing." If he loved her enough…

"This is my home. And it was yours too. Besides, we agreed to try the long-distance thing. But you called it quits as soon as your plane touched wheels on the ground."

"That isn't true." She'd wanted desperately to make the long-distance arrangement work. "As soon as I was out of sight, it was out of mind. You wouldn't answer your cell. I called it quits? You're the one who ran off with another woman before the Christmas lights were extinguished."

"What are you talking about?" Alex jerked sideways, throwing Mary against the back of the couch. "*You* wouldn't answer *my* calls." He leaped to a standing position, his eyes narrowed, and his nostrils flared. "There *wasn't* any other woman."

She matched his indignation and jumped to her feet. "That's not what your mother said." She lifted her chin with as much defiance as she could muster, considering his steadfast declaration.

Alex's mouth came open. Confusion rippled his face. His shock and disbelief appeared so genuine she wanted to crumple. Had she misunderstood? No, how could she? His mother's words were clear enough. "She said you went to California to be with Carrie." Now the tears were so close to the surface, she choked a sob.

"Oh my gosh!" Mary sat straight. "Oh! Oh!"

The shock on Alex's face morphed into an expression she could only describe as hilarity. With wide eyes and a broad smile, he guffawed. But it was short lived.

He dropped his chin. "Oh, no. No, no."

"Tell her, Bubba." Mary tugged on his hand hanging limp at his side.

Sadi's heart hammered her chest. Her watery eyes

cleared. Something strange was happening. Between Mary's rosy-cheeked, joyful expression and Alex's dejected body language, she couldn't fathom what.

Alex lifted his gaze and stared into her face. Still, he was speechless.

Mary elbowed his thigh. "Bubba. Snap out of it."

Nerves skittered up her neck. Her scalp went prickly. His intense stare was all she could see as if a fog closed around them. They were the only two people in the world.

He shook his head. "If only you'd answered my phone calls."

"If only you'd answered *my* calls," she countered.

"I would've, but… I can only guess you called during the confusion. Carina was hurt. My phone dropped from my pocket. I never got it back so we assumed it was somehow destroyed…on a street or crushed under a luggage cart at the airport. I tried to call you after Carina was settled. You wouldn't answer. I figured…"

"But your mom said—"

"Oh, for Pete's sake," his sister muttered, then touched her arm. "I'm Carrie."

Huh? She tore her gaze from Alex. Mary's beaming face lifted the fog.

"Sadi, listen. *I'm* Carrie."

Mary is Carrie?

Several gasps came from the direction of the fireplace. One of the three wise men chuckled.

What's so funny? "I don't understand."

"Of course you don't because this lughead won't explain." Mary rose, shaking her head. "Remember I told you I was in a car accident? It was right before Christmas. *The* Christmas Bubba says he was dumped. You were the dumper, huh?"

"I didn't dump him!"

"Then what?" The protective sister had her hands balled into fists on her hips. Sadi thought she just might get that punch in the nose.

"The job offer was monumental. We agreed to try it apart. Your brother wouldn't leave you, your family, at Christmas. We had no idea how it would work, but we made our promises. As soon as I was picked up from the airport, I was sucked into a whirlwind. I called when I could the first couple of days, but he wouldn't answer." She darted a glance at Alex. His eyes darkened. Sadi gulped air. "It didn't take me long to realize the fairy tale job was more like a bad dream."

"We were having our own bad dream." Alex trailed a finger down Mary's cheek.

"I see that now. But when I gave up on your cell and called your house, and your mom said…" She couldn't bring herself to repeat the sentence that changed her life.

"I've always called her Carina Ballerina, but her full name is Mary Carina. Mom calls her Carrie." His brows tipped downward with sadness. "I had to go to California with Mary to oversee her care."

All the air whooshed from her lungs. Her head spun. All this time…

"All this time." Alex echoed her thoughts.

Mary took each of their hands, placing Sadi's in Alex's, then stepped away.

"You came back," he said.

"Yes."

"Kiss her, stupid," one of the wise men cracked.

He drew her close.

She willingly fell against him. The kiss she'd only dreamed about came true.

It might never have ended, except the applause from the group around the fireplace had her giggling.

"I'm never letting you out of my sight again." He brushed another kiss across her mouth. "Merry Christmas, Sadi Anne."

Those words held true meaning for her now. Christmas could become her favorite time of year. "Merry Christmas, Alex."

OTHER BOOKS BY BRENDA

The MacKenzie Chronicles
Secrets of the Ravine, book 1
Mystery on Spirit Mountain, book 2
Curse of Wolf Falls, book 3

The Chocolate Martini Sisters Mysteries
Candy, Cigarettes, and Murder, book 1
Reading, Writing, and Murder, book 2
Cornbread, Ribs, and Murder, book 3

Wild Horse Peaks
The Art of Love and Murder
Southwest of Love and Murder
The Power of Love and Murder
The Deep Well of Love and Murder

Sleeping with the Lights On

The Morning After

Amanda in the Summer

Post-War Dreams

A Legacy of Love and Murder, a Sequel in The Wild Horse Peaks books

Sadi and Max Chapter Books
(writing as Brenda Sue and Sadi Belle)
Sadi and Max Have the Best Christmas in the Entire World
Sadi and Max to the Rescue

About the author…

Brenda Whiteside is the award-winning author of romantic suspense, romance, and cozy mystery. She writes children's books under the pen name, Brenda Sue and Sadi Belle. After living in six states and two countries, she and her husband have settled in Central Arizona. They share their home with a rescue dog named Amigo. While FDW fishes, Brenda writes.

To receive special offers, news about her latest books, and to be eligible for quarterly and year-end gifts that only members of BNG receive, join Brenda's Newsletter Group on her webpage.

Visit Brenda at https://www.brendawhiteside.com
Or on FaceBook: Brenda Whiteside
Or X: brendawhitesid2
She blogs and has guests on: Discover…